———————— ★ ————————

"You want Chinese?"

Peanuts Pianone liked Chinese food better than pasta and he counted on Tuttle's willingness to settle down with sweet-and-sour pork, fried rice of various kinds, egg rolls.

At the Toyota, Tuttle got out.

"The Orient Express?" Peanuts called.

Tuttle nodded. There seemed to be something in his car, as if someone had thrown a coat into the back seat. He opened the door and saw the girl's legs first, exposed because her skirt had ridden up her hips. Her sightless eyes studied the back seat. She was dead. Tuttle knew who she was. Sonya Bourke.

———————— ★ ————————

"Fans of McInerny's...will be delighted with this tale..."
—*Publishers Weekly*

"Father Roger Dowling...is quaint but not at all unbelievable."
—*Washington Post*

RALPH McINERNY

JUDAS PRIEST

W🌐RLDWIDE.®

TORONTO • NEW YORK • LONDON
AMSTERDAM • PARIS • SYDNEY • HAMBURG
STOCKHOLM • ATHENS • TOKYO • MILAN
MADRID • WARSAW • BUDAPEST • AUCKLAND

JUDAS PRIEST

A Worldwide Mystery/November 1994

First published by St. Martin's Press, Incorporated.

ISBN 0-373-26156-X

Printed in U.S.A.

For Laura and Jorge Garcia

ONE

MRS. MURKIN put the visitor in the front parlor and hurried back to the kitchen so she could be on the lookout for Father Dowling when he returned from saying the noon Mass. Forsythia bloomed along the walk leading from rectory to church, but it bloomed in vain as far as lifting Marie's spirits were concerned. She had faced some sticky situations in her years as housekeeper of the St. Hilary rectory, but the visitor in the front parlor posed a problem she had never before faced.

She had long since reached the age when, it is said, we have the face we deserve. Pale-blue eyes peered through glasses that required her to tip back her head as if about to receive communion in order to read anything. No jottings on the kitchen calendar came to her help, no reminder of a pastoral duty that might spare Father Dowling the embarrassment of talking to the visitor waiting for him in the front parlor.

The sensible thing would be to get rid of the man, serve lunch, and get on with the day. Of course she didn't for a minute think the pastor would do the sensible thing. It was the kind of thing she had to do for him. She dropped her head, let her eyes rise above her glasses, and whispered a prayer. Her prayer life consisted largely in bargaining with the Lord, which meant asking for things she didn't get. Nonetheless, her faith was strong and she remained convinced that checking in with God and His blessed saints was the wise thing to do.

The name Keegan stayed with her as an afterimage from looking at the calendar and she stopped. Was that the answer to her prayer? She picked up the phone to call Captain Keegan, but before she could dial, Father Dowling appeared on the walk, coming from the church.

Marie hung up the phone and scooted out the back door and down the porch steps, waving soundlessly at the priest. The pastor had stopped to look thoughtfully at the forsythia bush. Ha. He wasn't fooling Marie Murkin. He knew about as much about gardening as she did, which meant that if he took any more interest in that forsythia, it would wither and die.

Oh, why didn't he look toward the house? "Father," she cried in a whispered shout, "Father." Of course he didn't hear her. The only one who might was the man in the front parlor. Marie started along the walk toward the pastor, continuing to wave her arms like an idiot. She was halfway to him when he turned. He took a step backward and she realized she was still flapping her arms.

"Leaving the nest, Marie?"

"Father, you have a visitor."

"No reason for you to take flying lessons. Look at these flowers."

"That's forsythia."

"I wondered what it was called."

Was he serious? You never knew. "Does the name Bourke mean anything to you?"

"It does indeed."

"Thank God."

"There were four Bourkes in the seminary with me and one day the rector suggested that the place was becoming tubercular. Too Bourke-ular." He waited. "It's a joke, Marie."

"This may be one of them."

She had his undivided attention at last. They started toward the house and the smells of cooking came to meet them from the kitchen. A pained look came over the priest's face.

"That does not smell like a Lenten meal, Marie."

Lenten meals shouldn't smell—or taste, for that matter—in Father Dowling's book, but Marie took her duty to be the care and feeding of the pastor so he would have the strength to carry out his duties. As often as not, when his duty called, she considered it to be her duty to interpose herself between Father Dowling and overly demanding parishioners. In the case of visitors like the man waiting in the parlor, it was Marie's view that Father Dowling had no obligation whatsoever to see him.

"There aren't two hundred calories in a serving."

"You're talking dieting, I'm talking fasting. What about Bourkes?"

"This one is named Christopher."

"Chris Bourke!"

"He's here. In the parlor. I wanted to warn you. I told him you were out, but he knew you were saying Mass and said he'd be glad to wait."

"He can have lunch with me. Two hundred calories should be enough to share."

Marie's worst fears were realized. She planted herself in the middle of the walk, blocking his progress.

"You are not going to ask that man to have a lunch I prepared in the dining room of this house."

When Father Dowling raised his brows, the right one always rose higher than the left. Once more he stepped back, this time to make a deep bow. "I hadn't heard of your appointment as pastor, Marie, let alone your ordination. My congratulations."

"Stop it. Do you know who he is or don't you?"

"Chris Bourke? Of course. We were in the seminary together."

"Well, you have nothing in common anymore."

"Aha. Is that it? But Marie, the damage is done. The neighbors might have seen you let him in. You've already disgraced us and I'll just have to make the best of it."

Sometimes he made her so mad she could scream. He took her hands and deftly wheeled around her and bounced up the porch steps. He held the kitchen door open after he had gone in and Marie took her time, let him stand there being gallant, she didn't care.

In the doorway, she put her hand on his arm and said in a fierce whisper, "Now if he were a divorced man, it would be a different story, wouldn't it?"

"In the parlor?"

"Talk to him there," she urged. "Don't ask him to lunch."

"It'll give you a chance to poison his food."

And he sailed on down the hallway to the parlor, his cassock whipping at his legs. What an infuriating man he could be. On his good days he was the best pastor St. Hilary's had ever had, but when he was bad, oh, he was horrid.

TWO

THE VISITOR HAD PULLED one of the wooden armchairs to the window and sat in profile, chin in his hand, looking out the window. He might have been a confessor listening to the accumulated sins of the world. This somber thought was encouraged by his expression, one suggestive of an almost total depression and confusion. Roger Dowling stood in the doorway and cleared his throat, but Chris Bourke did not turn. The lemon-yellow sport coat and tan slacks suggested a climate warmer than Fox River, Illinois, and Chris's tan, too, suggested elsewhere. Odd. The last Roger Dowling had heard, Chris and his wife were still broadcasting from Chicago.

"Chris," he said, crossing the parlor to his visitor.

"Roger!" The tragic expression fell away and was replaced by a smile that could only be called professional. "Sorry to just burst in on you like this."

"Nonsense. You're just in time for lunch. I've only now come from saying the noon Mass."

"A noon Mass," Chris murmured. "Yes, your housekeeper told me."

He might have gone over to the church and come into the sacristy after the Mass was over, but he had chosen to wait in the rectory. Perhaps he wanted to give Marie the chance to do what she had done, warn the pastor of who awaited him.

"Thank you, but no, Roger. What I want mainly is to set a time when we could get together. I want very much to talk with you."

"Why not now?"

"Do you really mean it?"

Chris seemed to be searching his face for clues on how to read this reception. Had he expected to be shunned, turned away, given the brush-off? Marie must have shown her shock at seeing him on the doorstep of a Roman Catholic rectory, and he would think her attitude was the pastor's as well. What was his attitude? Roger realized he didn't know. For the moment he was willing simply to treat Chris as he would anyone else he had known in the seminary. Like Phil Keegan.

In the dining room, Chris stood behind the chair Roger pointed him to, looking around. "Nothing has changed. Noon Mass, a housekeeper, a rectory like this. Roger, you're living in a time warp."

"Let's say grace."

Chris dutifully bowed his head and Roger began, *"Benedic nos, domine..."* Saying it in Latin was pushing it, of course, but Chris thought he was living in a time warp, so maybe he expected it. Halfway through, Chris's lips began to move as he sought and found the words.

"Amazing what you remember," he said, when they were seated and Marie entered with a trout she had burned in what she insisted was Cajun style.

"Like riding a bicycle," Roger said. "I was at a funeral a week ago, old Monsignor Whitney, and when the celebrant began the *Salve Regina* at the grave site, the young priests didn't know it. Imagine that. Can they say Mass in Latin? That's the question.''

"Do you?"

"Once a week. The *novus ordo*. The first Mass Sunday morning."

"Do many come?"

"Seven o'clock and the church is packed. Many are there for aesthetic reasons or to make some statement of discontent, but I think that will pass as it becomes less of an oddity."

"I thought the whole thing had unraveled, Roger."

"Well, the sleeve of care is not what it was, nor is the Church. But the public stuff, what you read in the paper, is only a small fraction of what's going on. Probably the least representative. How long has it been, Chris?''

Despite the prelude, the question seemed to embarrass his guest. He glanced at Marie, who was making one of her swooping tours of the dining room to see if anything was needed.

"Twenty years. Going on twenty-one." He shook his head. "I can't get used to thinking of my life in terms of decades."

"Like a rosary."

"You're still saying that, I'll bet."

"Most people are, Chris."

"Are you serious?"

He was serious. Prior to Lenten Masses there was the recital of the rosary in the church and almost everyone who came for Mass came a little earlier for that. The truth was that Roger Dowling was somewhat surprised himself recounting this. It was hard not to be affected by the general media impression of a Church in revolt, everyone unhappy and demanding changes, specified and unspecified. Catholic politicians didn't help, of course. Imagine what would happen to Jewish senators and representatives if they voted against aid to Israel. And there was something to the description of St. Hilary parish in Fox River as unrepresentative. Once Roger Dowling would have regarded his parish as the diocesan equivalent of Siberia, a place to exile troublesome or ineffectual priests. Maybe others still did think of it that way. But he knew it to be the place where he had, after a choppy period, regained the sense of his vocation. St. Hilary's might not have been the goal he had dreamed of when he and Chris were seminarians at Mundelein, but it was where he belonged.

"Getting here wasn't easy," he said to Chris.

"I thought you were meant for a miter, Roger."

"So did I."

He had returned from Catholic University with a doctorate in canon law and been assigned to the archdiocesan marriage tribunal. Almost from the beginning, people had said what Chris had said, that he would eventually become a bishop, first an auxiliary in Chicago, and then, who knew? Clerical ambition is an odd thing. The pope is called the servant of the servants of God, making the top the bottom, but there are other aspects of the difference between simple priest and bishop, just as there is a hierarchy of jobs held by priests. The Church could start looking like a corporation and the desire for upward mobility seemed part of the system. But Roger Dowling had been unable to take the daily attrition of the marriage court in stride. Hearing confessions is tough enough, that constant whispered account of the weaknesses of human beings, but the failed marriages that end up in an ecclesiastical court will almost never find their remedy there. What could be more tragic than to confront again and again spouses who want to be rid of one another and to have to tell them that they had joined themselves for life? Increasingly Roger had taken refuge in drink, perhaps unconsciously disqualifying himself for his job. He ended up in a sanatorium in Wisconsin. He had come to St. Hilary's from there. Sometimes he felt that it was only here, in this western outpost of the archdiocese, that his priesthood had begun. Had Chris heard none of this, or was he merely being kind?

Marie cleared away the dishes, leaving a carafe of coffee on the table.

"We can talk here or in my study."

For answer, Chris pushed back from the table. Marie's presence was almost palpable. She would not have described what she was doing as eavesdropping. On the contrary, she considered it part of her job to keep informed on everything that was going on in the parish, particularly in the rectory. So she could be of help. Marie had everything but Holy Orders, but she was merciless with those who agitated for women's ordination.

"You're for women's subordination, is that it?" Roger teased her sometimes.

"What was good enough for Our Lady is good enough for me," the housekeeper would say primly and march into her kitchen.

Now when they stood and Roger had given thanks, in English, Marie came to the doorway and looked in. Her expression seemed to ask if she had done something to offend.

"We'll take this coffee into the study, Marie."

"Just call if you want anything else."

And then, for the first time, Marie permitted herself to look at their guest and her expression suggested that she would not be surprised to see a pair of black wings sprout from his shoulder blades.

In the study, Roger put Chris in the green leather chair Phil Keegan considered his own and sat behind the desk. Chris was looking around the room, sniffing ostentatiously.

"Do you smoke hams in here?"

"Tobacco, mainly."

"I'm shocked." But he said it with a smile.

"I have cigars and cigarettes. I don't imagine you'd want to borrow one of my pipes."

"Get thou behind me, Satan."

"Smoking remains one of the compensatory pleasures of the celibate life."

"Along with drinking?"

"I quit that."

"Then smoke, Roger. Smoke."

He needed neither permission nor encouragement, but the pipe tasted even better as he listened to Chris tell him of the awful time he had quitting.

"For over a year, I was sneaking them, so my followers wouldn't know I was still doing what I was insisting they stop doing. It wasn't wholly hypocrisy, however. I fully intended to stop. And I did."

"Good for you."

"You don't sound as if you meant that."

It did seem strange to be commending Chris Bourke, the self-described champion of hedonism, for his asceticism, and he said so.

"Asceticism? I don't consider killing myself a pleasure to be forgone."

"No dangerous pleasures?"

Chris leaned forward, clamping his knees in his hands. "Roger, I appreciate your willingness to see me. It wasn't easy for me to come here. I almost hoped you'd be diplomatically absent. I wouldn't have blamed you."

The damage Chris Bourke had done his fellow priests was incalculable. Not only had he left the priesthood, he had done so in a noisy way, condemning the Church he claimed had oppressed him throughout his life. Few Catholics would have recognized their Church as the Gulag he described, and fewer priests found their memories of the seminary and of priestly life at all like Chris Bourke's. His bombastic exit had made him a darling of the media—in those days, such statements made by an ordained priest were still man-bites-dog stuff—and for months he'd appeared on talk shows, local and national, telling viewers what a dreadful thing the Catholic Church was. But it was his lurid attack on celibacy that drew talk-show hosts as nectar draws bees. Chris blandly admitted that he himself had not been true to his promise of celibacy and infuriated his fellow priests—although, since he had repudiated his priesthood as well as his Church, perhaps this was not an accurate locution—by claiming that it was doubtful ten percent of the clergy led celibate lives.

"The ones over seventy," he added with a smile.

One newspaper story told of the coaching he had undergone prior to his television appearances, and indeed there was a professional polish to his performance from the very beginning. After a year of plucking a single negative string, he gained new media life by advocating what he called EH—Enlightened Hedonism—and his persuasive powers became even more palpable.

Like other priests, particularly those who had known him in the seminary, Roger Dowling had followed the beginnings of Chris Bourke's secular career with fascination and dread. Tragic as the loss of faith must seem to any believer, there was the added note of treachery, of savaging with remarks he must have known were false when he left the institution he had left. The fact that his apostasy was so lucrative should, or so Father Dowling thought, have given Chris pause. He was being rewarded by the Prince of this World. What did it profit a man if he gained the whole world and suffered the loss of his own soul? Chris Bourke had dismissed that vision of life, of course, but could he remove it thoroughly from his consciousness?

His positive phase scarcely begun, Chris announced that he would marry. His intended bride was, inevitably perhaps, a former nun, a beautiful woman

hardly more than a girl, who credited Chris Bourke
with enabling her to see the light. Janet Gray's gratitude that she had freed herself from the convent while
still young enough to enjoy her liberty brought a ra-
diant smile to her televised face. She and Chris began
to make joint appearances and audiences found aph-
rodisiac their revelations about the fierce sexuality the
Church had tried to suppress. Rumors of their relationship began, so that the marriage had a kind of in-
evitability in it. Janet, it was to emerge, was already
pregnant, and in those pre-abortion days she had accepted her fate. Chris made an honest woman of her,
but after *Roe v. Wade* they both said that, under the
new dispensation, it was doubtful Janet would have
borne her child. They said this while dandling on their
knee the golden-haired daughter who combined the
best features of her parents. It was best to think that
they could not possibly mean it, but how could one
tell?

"How old is your daughter now?"

"She is why I have come, Roger."

"How so?"

Chris looked at his hands, he lifted his eyes and tried
to smile, then the expression he had worn in the parlor before he realized Roger Dowling was standing in
the doorway once more took possession of his face.

"Sonya wants to enter the convent."

THREE

CRAIG WILHELMS had been in the television ministry
for fifteen years, largely in supporting capacities, but
still in a position to learn all the skills of the genre before becoming a vice president of EH and, effectively, the manager of the careers of Chris Bourke and
Janet Gray. The first time he saw the former priest on
television had been inadvertent. One sleepless night he
had lain in bed, flicking the remote control, checking
the opposition, so to speak, ranking the other preachers in comparison with the Reverend Biggs, his then
employer. But of course there was no set of agreed-
upon standards. Sometimes Craig thought of TV
evangelists as like the male singers of his youth, each
with his own following, no two entirely alike, yet all of
them somehow the same. This theory helped reconcile him to the Reverend Biggs, who, he had come increasingly to think, either didn't believe a thing he
preached or, worse, did, and considered his salvation
or damnation already settled, so what did it matter
how he behaved? A press of the button and there was
Father Christopher Bourke, as he was still styled. ("I
hope to earn that title soon," Bourke said with his
boyish grin. "Biologically.") Much of the man's message seemed to be that religion had kept him out of the
sack, at least legitimately, and now he intended to

make up for what he had been missing. Craig was still married to Louise then, and it was difficult to match Bourke's exuberant account of sexuality with the everyday routine of married life. Bourke seemed to think that the rest of the world had been engaged in a continual orgy while he writhed repressed in his narrow celibate's bed. Listening to him, Craig imagined the man spreading this message in a kind of parody of a television ministry. The thought kept revolving in his mind, and two days later, having talked with Bourke on the phone, he was on the plane to Chicago.

They began small, taping in a Chicago studio, no audience, just Chris and Janet, and Craig as straight man, eliciting incredible remarks from the former nun and priest, a call to the untrammeled pursuit of pleasure. Effortlessly the two put their X-rated message in homiletic tones, making being bad seem a way of being good. Perhaps only a couple with their peculiar backgrounds could have gotten away with it. There were a few protests, except from enraged Catholics, but the defense of the show became the freedom to practice religion according to one's own conscience. Memories of the convent or priesthood continued to add zest to the mix, but over the years EH became a positive program. Syndicated to an ever-growing number of stations, it was only a matter of time before Bourke had his own channel and EH was big business. By then people fought over tickets to be part of the live studio audience, the cassettes and videotapes were best-sellers, other performers were added. There were ex-priests and -nuns by the dozen who ap-

plied, but wisely they steered away from them. That
would have been to water the wine. Cecilia, a former
call girl, spoke frankly of the mechanics of sexual ecstasy and a dwarflike avuncular old man discoursed on
senior sex. Lesbians and homosexual men were given,
if not equal time, certainly a noticeable fraction of air
time. It fit in with the general message of EH—pleasure is nature's way of telling us it's okay. Bourke developed what might have been called the theology of
the movement, since the message was that everything
that had been sought in vain in religious belief could
be had through Enlightened Hedonism.

If there was a cynical bone in Chris Bourke's body,
Craig was unaware of it. Through the years he had
expected Chris to reveal, however indirectly, that he
knew what he was doing was parasitic on his priestly
past, that long after the shock of recognizing that the
man saying these incredible things about sexuality had
been a priest wore off, the rhetoric of the shows still
fed on that of the evangelists who were urging the
masses to salvation. The simple fact seemed to be that
Chris believed what he was saying. And Janet was no
different. How else could they have used their own
daughter in discussions of the sexuality of infants?
There on national television was little Sonya in her
bath, innocently exploring herself, while her parents
commented on the autoerotic implications of what she
was doing. Desi and Lucy had written pregnancy into
their scripts and included children in shows, but this
use of little Sonya was something else entirely. Only
Craig seemed to find it tasteless and exploitative.

Not that he said so. By then he was so intimately involved in the whole effort he couldn't claim the necessary distance to pass judgment on what they were doing. Besides, aside from the cascades of cash that all but inundated them, there were tons of testimonials from viewers freed from repression and bondage by the frankness of Janet and Chris. The two had even considered being filmed as they made love, the better to convey to their audience how liberated they were from the oppressive constraints of Christian morality. They actually made a home video, performing for a fixed camera. It was when Craig brought that home to show Louise that she walked out. A life lived for pleasure becomes boring, finally, or so it had become for Craig and his wife. Children? Why tie themselves down? Besides, it would seem a concession to the notion that children are the justification of sexual activity. Chris might continue to laud the infinite variety of sexual expression, but Craig and Louise got bogged down in finitude. Craig began to have dreams of being in a monastery; solitude and lack of sex exercised an almost sensual attraction. He daydreamed of desert saints, punishing their bodies, turning their minds to God. That was his real problem, finally; he just couldn't stop believing in God. He decided he had to confess that to Chris.

"Of course you do. You have no choice. God is just another name for what we really want."

"Jesus?"

"Jesus, Buddha, Isis, they're all the same, symbolizations of the object of desire. Do you realize how sexy mystical literature is?"

"Tell me about Catholicism."

"Do you mean it?"

"Where I grew up, it was only the Whore of Babylon."

So Chris told him about Catholicism, concisely, in an orderly way, right out of Vatican II. It was the first time Craig had been able to imagine Chris as a priest. He must have been good at it, but that should come as no surprise. He had never really changed professions. He had gone after strange gods, was all, but he was still a missioner. Those sessions on Catholicism had been fatal to Craig's attempted disbelief. He began to attend Mass in Holy Name Cathedral, very early in the morning, feeling like Nicodemus, imitating the strange gestures, kneelings and risings of those around him, fascinated by what was going on at the distant altar, sharing the hushed expectation, believing it all before he was quite clear what it all was.

Thus he had become a closet Catholic and been torn in two by the contradiction of remaining with EH. His fear was no longer that he would be discovered by someone else. The great danger was that he would drive himself mad by the conflict between his inner conviction and his participation in the televised effort to convince millions that their destiny lay in their genitals.

And then one day he turned around at Mass to give
the sign of peace to the other worshippers and found
himself looking into the wondering gaze of Sonya
Bourke.

FOUR

"IS IT TRUE about Chris Bourke coming to see you?" Phil Keegan asked, up to adjust the television, his back to Roger Dowling.

"Do you remember him?"

"Marie was pretty upset."

And so, by his tone, was Phil Keegan. Would he have known Chris? Phil had attended Quigley but had been undone by his inability to learn Latin. Chris Bourke might have been in the minor seminary at that time. But of course the Chris Bourke Phil knew was the renegade priest who had made a career out of attacking the Church. There might be Catholics who were unbothered by Chris Bourke and his bride, but Phil Keegan was not among them. Who is more loyal to the Church than a former seminarian? Phil had gone on to the army and MP duty and, when he returned to civilian life, became a policeman. Now as captain of detectives of the Fox River Police, a widower, he had renewed his acquaintance with Roger Dowling. Often, as tonight, the two men got together for a televised game. The White Sox were playing in Sarasota and the two Cubs fans grudgingly settled down to watch.

"There's more beer, Phil."

"Later."

For Phil to postpone a beer while watching sports suggested that he had in mind a serious conversation. Roger might tease Marie when she pried into pastoral business but that wouldn't work with Phil.

"What did he want?" Phil let the words emerge like smoke signals.

"To talk."

"Yeah?"

"It was quite a surprise to find him here."

"Marie says you invited him to lunch."

"Too bad you weren't here. You could have met him."

"I wouldn't sit in the same room with that son of a bitch," Phil said in sudden anger. "Roger, why would you give the time of day to a man who abandoned his vocation, married a nun, and made a career out of lying about the Church?"

"He came to me, Phil."

"You'd talk to anyone who showed up at the door? Hitler, maybe?"

"Him most of all. When he was still alive, I mean."

"You know what I mean."

"I know what you mean. The conversation was confidential, Phil."

It was the ultimate trump and Phil knew it, even though he glared at Roger as if trying to figure out whether the pastor of St. Hilary's would invoke confidentiality simply to avoid a difficult question. He turned his glare on the TV and watched three innings more or less in silence. Only a bases-loaded triple play distracted him from the rage Marie's gossiping about

Chris Bourke's visit had built up in him. Roger wished he could confide in someone else the incredible point of that visit.

FOR SEVERAL DAYS he had pondered the irony of Chris's situation. What does a professional apostate do when his only child announces she is going to enter a convent?

"Will you talk to her, Roger?" Chris had asked.

"You mean talk her out of it?"

"If I wanted someone to do that, there are any number of nuns I could have enlisted. But it wouldn't have worked. Why should she listen to women who complain how dreadful their life is? Obviously it's not dreadful enough to leave or they would. Sonya would discount that kind of thing in a minute. I know you'll talk straight to her."

"Where did she get this idea?"

"God only knows." He made a face. "So to speak. Will you talk to her?"

"If she wants me to."

"That's part of the problem, Roger. If I ask her to come to Fox River to talk to you, she won't do it. She'll figure it's part of our campaign to stop her."

"What does Janet think of this?"

"Imagine. Of course it's pretty obvious what motivates Sonya."

"Oh?"

"It's a way of getting back at us, punishing us. She knows our backgrounds, she knows our public stance. What better way to hurt us?"

"You mean the publicity?"

"That would be the least of it."

"You'd have someone to pray for you."

Chris laughed halfheartedly. "Sure. But you can do that. I get letters all the time, nuns praying for my conversion. Those are the nice letters."

"If it's just a way of hurting you, it's not very likely she'd go ahead and do it."

"Roger, I don't think she really knows what she's doing. She isn't even a Catholic. How can she become a nun?"

"Was she baptized?"

"No." He looked pensive. "Not that I know of. As far as I can make out, she thinks she's a Catholic because we were."

"Has she talked to anyone?"

"A priest? She won't say. The more questions we ask, the more weapons we hand her. She knows what would hurt us."

"Chris, you must remember how you felt when you entered the seminary."

"It's not the same thing, I was raised in the Church, I'd been an altar boy, my family was religious. For me it was a natural step. Now, if I had decided to become a Buddhist monk, that would be like what Sonya is doing to us."

"I don't see why you want me to talk to her. Obviously whatever she might tell me would be between her and me. Even more obviously, I can't promise to warn her away from a religious vocation."

"Just explain it to her. Tell her what it is. What it would demand of her. Tell her she has to be a Catholic, for Pete's sake, and that means instruction..." He stopped and slapped his forehead with an open hand. "This is nuts. Rationally, I know she'll do nothing, but I can't put it out of my mind."

"What if she were to enter the convent?"

Chris looked away. "I'd rather see her dead."

"That's pretty strong."

"I mean it, Roger. You know what I think of things."

"I know what you say."

"And mean. In all due respect, Roger, I find it hard to believe that a man of your intelligence really thinks all that stuff is true. I don't think I ever did, not really. Of course I thought it was just a temptation when as an altar boy I couldn't bring myself to think the bread and wine literally turned into Jesus. I should have listened to myself then. I stopped saying daily Mass my second year out, because it was agony saying the words of consecration and not believing anything was happening. Sundays were different, that was a show, a public event, my sermon. Finally I decided to stop fooling myself."

"Meaning you lost your faith."

"If I ever had it. But what is faith except the determination to say what you know is false is true."

"It is the substance of things hoped for."

"Saint Paul."

"Good for you."

"Oh, I still have it all at my fingertips, Roger. More than I had before I left."

"Know your enemy?"

"If you believed what I do, wouldn't you feel an obligation to free people from the grip of a myth?"

"I have my own obligations, Chris."

"Talk to her anyway, Roger. Please. I want to be sure that she gets the straight dope. I just don't believe the reality would be attractive."

"Has she ever visited a convent?"

"I doubt it."

BUT ROGER DOWLING would find that Chris knew very little of the daughter he wanted to keep out of the convent.

Sonya was a senior at Northwestern and Roger drove in to Evanston to meet her after he finally got through to her on the phone.

"Your father came to see me," he said, after telling her who he was. "We were in the seminary together."

"You're still a priest?"

"By the grace of God. Of course you can't really stop being a priest."

"What do you mean?"

He told her of the ordination ceremony and the Church's use of "Thou art a priest forever, according to the Order of Melchisedech."

"Even after you die?"

"Yes."

And that, as it happened, was why she agreed to see him. Their rendezvous was the coffee shop of the Hotel Carrington. Meeting her was like seeing her mother years ago, although as they talked he saw traces of Chris in her too. She was a very pretty girl but seemed to dress to de-emphasize the fact. His Roman collar surprised her and he thought he detected embarrassment as they went to a table. They ordered coffee and then she put her hands on the table and smiled at him almost wistfully.

"I've seen a picture of Dad wearing one of those." She meant the collar.

"Would you tell me more of what you were saying on the phone?"

She meant about the priesthood, its permanence. He repeated what he had said.

"But men leave. My father left."

"One can be laicized but that doesn't remove Holy Orders. The sacrament leaves an indelible mark."

He might have been speaking to a Martian. She had a very vague notion of sacraments. But that did not divert her from what had occurred to her.

"You mean my father is still a priest?"

"Yes."

"Is my mother still a nun?"

"That's not a sacrament."

"You mean she isn't."

He had no way of knowing if Janet Gray had been released from her vows, but he said, "Being a nun isn't like being a priest."

"That's weird, isn't it, a man who's still a priest doing what he does?"

"I'm not talking of what he thinks or believes, only about what is the case."

"Meaning what you believe."

"Meaning what is true."

"You think that about people who divorce, too, don't you? That they're still really married."

There is little less interesting than religion at the level of canon law, and it was as a canon lawyer that he knew this. If Sonya thought Catholicism was exhausted by the laws expressive of it, this was not going to be much of a conversation.

"Your father says you want to be a nun."

"I figured he'd told you. Are you supposed to talk me out of it?"

"Could I?"

She sat back as their coffee was served. When the waitress was gone, she looked at him for a moment. "Would you try?"

"I told him I wouldn't. He didn't ask me to."

"Then why did he go to you?"

"I knew him in the seminary."

"I'll bet you haven't seen him in years."

"Only on television."

"Television!" She picked up her cup and sipped. The coffee was very hot and she reached desperately for her water.

"Are you just teasing your parents about going into the convent?"

"That's how it started."

"Tell me about it."

She took a deep breath, then sat in silence for a moment. "All my life I've been hearing how awful religion is. Maybe it is, how would I know, but if what my parents do is the alternative, what's the choice, really? Either way, it seemed just a way of kidding yourself. The difference was, when do you get paid, here or there? The first time I went into a church I was practically disguised, sunglasses, a babushka. As if anyone cared. I just meant to peek but after a while I sat in a pew and watched people. It was a church in the Loop and people kept coming and going, kneeling down with all their bundles around them, making the rounds of the statues, lighting candles. I couldn't believe it. But I found I could stare without anyone staring back, so I stayed for more than an hour. Of course the strangeness went away after a bit. I didn't know what altar to look at for a while but then I settled on the central one. Maybe I noticed the special lamp that first time, I don't know, but I wouldn't have known what it meant then."

"What does it mean?"

"That Jesus is there."

"Do you believe that?"

"Yes."

"When did that start?"

"The first time. When I got up to go. I started to turn toward the door and couldn't. My eyes wouldn't leave the little gold house on the altar. The tabernacle. Then I realized why. He was in there."

"Who had told you?"

"No one."

The coming of faith, like its going, is shrouded in mystery. Apparently Sonya had been granted the gift of faith before she really knew what its object was.

"I bought some pamphlets in the back of the church but they didn't make much sense. It was Daddy's books that explained it all to me."

"And now you want to go into the convent."

"I made up my mind long ago that I never wanted to get married. I am so sick of talk about sex. My parents are accused of thinking people are animals but I can't imagine any animal being as fascinated by sexuality as my parents are. After I started visiting churches I saw the point of that decision."

"You should visit a convent and see what it's like."

"Where can I find one?"

She really didn't know. She seemed genuinely surprised to hear that Chicago was full of convents.

"Have you talked with your mother?"

"She said she'd kill me if I mentioned it again. I told her she should have had an abortion when she had the chance. I thought she'd kill me then and there."

FIVE

PHIL TOLD HIMSELF it was charity, turning the other cheek, walking that extra mile, but no matter how he thought of it, he agreed with Marie. It was scandalous of Roger to admit a guy like Chris Bourke to the rectory, let alone invite him for lunch. *What if I'd gone to his Mass that day?* Phil thought. *What if I'd gone into the sacristy and been invited to lunch and then Roger asked Bourke to join us, what would I have done? Walk out?* If he had stayed it would only have been because Roger put him on the spot. He could not have eaten anything sitting at the same table with a heretic who had made a fortune telling lies about the Church. He would have made some excuse and got out of there.

Roger couldn't have done that, maybe, but why did he have to pretend there was nothing especially strange about welcoming Bourke? What did that bastard want with Roger anyway? A dramatic thought suddenly occurred to Phil. What, if after all these years, Chris Bourke wanted to come back to the fold!

What a sensation that would make! If that's what was going on, Roger's actions made sense. But when Phil tried the idea on Cy Horvath, the big lieutenant shook his head.

"Why not?"

"It's only a rumor. No one dares print the story first, but then the media have always protected those two. Besides, if he were just fooling around with another woman, it would fit in with his line of guff."

"What the hell are you talking about?"

"Janet and Chris Bourke are headed for a divorce. The big question is, how will they divide up the boodle?"

For Cy this amounted to a speech, and when he said something once, he considered it said. Phil looked into the matter himself, doing something he really hated to do, talk to a goddamn reporter. Tetzel drank like a fish, slurping down four beers while Keegan got the story out of him in the bar across from the courthouse.

"Why haven't you written this up?"

"I have. They won't print it, not yet anyway."

"But it's true?"

"Is the pope Polish?"

Tetzel was a smart ass, a fallen-away Unitarian, whatever that meant. He thought religion came down to the Bible-thumpers on the tube, who reminded him of public television during one of its fund drives.

"Those two getting a divorce is like Hugh Hefner getting married."

"I don't get you."

"The perfect partners, permanent playmates, that was the line. Oh, sure, he might try a little strange now and then, nothing serious, just to add a little zest to life and show how broad-minded they were. 'Broad'-

minded. He certainly is. He never has anything else on his mind.''

Keegan checked it out, he had Cy keep his ear to the ground, the story seemed to be true. The great fear was that this meant the end of the television show, maybe the whole enterprise would just collapse. Well, the two of them had made enough money already, enough to fight over, if it came to that. No one expected Janet to settle for some fraction of the pot and fade into the twilight.

"What do a couple of sex fiends do when they retire, Cy?"

"No idea."

"I can't imagine talking about my wife that way, can you?"

"Maybe once."

Good old Cy. The thought of him and the missus together was like mating porpoises. Good God, that's the effect Chris Bourke had on people. Keegan was ashamed of himself, thinking such thoughts of Cy and his wife. But if Keegan shocked himself, the realization that Bourke had been ordained a priest was more shocking still. It seemed diabolical to scandalize the faithful the way that man did. There were always some priests who from time to time did something out of the way, but to make a career out of losing your faith was something new, at least to Phil Keegan. But then the past twenty-five years had been strange ones all around so far as the Roman Catholic Church went. When Keegan left the seminary, he had been crushed, feeling cut off from the one life he had really wanted.

Now it seemed providential that he had been unable to master Latin and had had to leave. How in the world did Roger Dowling remain so calm while all around him what had seemed rock-solid and eternal crumbled?

"There's trouble in paradise, Roger."

"Oh?"

"The Bourkes."

"How so?"

Had Bourke come to Roger with his troubles about Janet? Roger just looked at him and said nothing.

"I can tell you what I know."

"I'm all ears."

Roger gave no indication while he listened whether the Bourkes's troubles were new to him or not, and that took some of the fun out of it, wondering if he was telling Roger old news—or, worse, telling him far less than he already knew.

"Gossip," Roger said when he was done.

Phil shook his head. "No. Tetzel swears to it, and Cy checked it out."

"They've had a longer run than many such couples."

"Wouldn't it be something if they both came back, Roger, and publicly admitted they'd been wrong?"

"Don't count on it, Phil."

Count on it? Phil drove the whole thing out of his mind.

Two days later the Bourkes in a panic announced that their daughter was missing.

SIX

TUTTLE SAT AT HIS DESK eating shrimp fried rice from a polystyrene container with a plastic spoon, his Irish tweed hat pushed back to facilitate feeding himself. On his desk was a cup of tea cooled. It didn't matter. Half the tea you drank was lukewarm, when you thought about it. Having wolfed down his midday meal, Tuttle tossed the containers into the wastebasket and looked across the room to where Peanuts was working away on a double-dip strawberry cone, eating it with deliberate slowness, childishly wanting his food to outlast Tuttle's.

"So what's the word on Sonya Bourke?"

Peanuts shrugged. For Tuttle at least it was an open question whether Peanuts was stupid or shrewd. Others had settled the matter long ago, and not in Peanuts's favor. But not everyone knew the man as well as Tuttle did. If Tuttle had any friend, it was Peanuts, and more often than even Tuttle would have admitted, Peanuts had been helpful to him. Critics might say he had done this by accident rather than design. Tuttle was willing to leave these niceties of interpretation to others. At the moment, he was waiting to see what lead Peanuts might give him on the Bourke girl.

When the Bourkes had shown up on the news the night before with the shocking announcement about their daughter, holding hands like a couple of kids, looking bewildered into the camera, Tuttle had hit the buttons on the VCR and taped it. How many times had he played those couple of minutes over, attentive to every word and intonation? His first notion had been that it was some kind of publicity stunt. The Bourkes had to be the biggest con artists Chicago had ever known, they were either loved or hated, no one was indifferent to them, and Tuttle would not have put past them a hoked-up story about their missing daughter as a way to boost their ratings. But after he had all but memorized the words and could close his eyes and run the tape from memory, he was convinced they were sincere. Their daughter was missing. Whether or not she had been kidnapped, as Janet Gray suggested, was another thing. How long had the kid been gone? They really weren't sure. They hadn't seen her for three days and she could have been gone longer.

"Have you received a ransom note?"

Janet looked at Chris, who shook his head. "Not yet." He addressed the camera. "Get in touch with me, whoever you are. I promise it will be confidential. Let my daughter go."

Inevitably the stations had run old tapes of the Bourkes blandly saying Janet would have gotten an abortion if that had been legal at the time she became pregnant. Children hadn't been part of the bargain she and Chris had entered into. There was an unconvincing braggadocio in those resurrected clips, as if the Bourkes had meant to cause shock rather than say what they really felt. Could any parents talk that way about their child and mean it? A lump formed in Tuttle's throat as he thought of his own paternal parent. His father had at great sacrifice paid Tuttle's way through law school, night school, almost every course taken twice, sweated out the years during which Tuttle had taken the bar exam every chance he got, finally squeaking through, a full-fledged lawyer at last. Shortly thereafter, as if exhausted by his son's labors, Tuttle senior had died. He was immortalized now in the name of the firm, Tuttle & Tuttle. It seemed a small tribute to a man who had retained such confidence in his son, despite consistently marginal performance.

With such a model of parental love, Tuttle was horrified anew to see those old tapes of the Bourkes, and even though he knew they couldn't possibly have meant that about their daughter, it was awful that they would even say it for the sake of effect.

Tuttle was disappointed that Peanuts had nothing to tell him, but it was worth the price of the double-dip cone to find out that the police had no leads.

"Are they working on it?"

Peanuts turned his hand back and forth.

"Don't they believe it?"

Peanuts smiled. That had to be it. The police were not convinced Sonya was missing, at least not in any way that involved them. Tuttle rose, tipped his hat over his eyes, waited for Peanuts to stand. It was time to mosey around and see what he could find out. Believing as he did that the Bourkes were sincere, he could get a head start on the case.

It was Tuttle's practice to keep his eye open for the main chance, a turn of events that spelled opportunity to the shrewd, and he had a good feeling about the missing Bourke girl. Bourke had practically promised any kidnapper a blank check, so he should be equally generous to anyone who located the girl, let alone brought her home safe and sound. The only question was how to proceed, and Officer Peanuts Pianone could be of no help to him there.

At the courthouse, Tuttle went into the newsroom and sipped a cup of coffee while he flipped through the papers, his ear cocked for any talk about Sonya Bourke. But all the talk was about the Sox opener the following day.

"Too cheap to pay a quarter for your own newspaper, Tuttle?" Tetzel clapped him on the back, a little harder than required.

"I'm looking for your story on Sonya Bourke."

"You won't find it. We ran a wire-service account of their TV performance and that's it. The whole thing is a pack of shit."

"You sure?"

"I'm sure. My editor's sure. Take a look at the *Trib* and the *Sun-Times*. Royko wrote about it, but things are slow."

"The Bourkes looked like they meant it to me."

"You're a lawyer, Tuttle. Credulous. A sucker for a line of bull. It's a smoke screen."

"Yeah?"

Tetzel grabbed his arm and pulled him close. His whisper could have been heard in the hallway. "They're breaking up, Tuttle. Maybe the girl's trying to keep them together. Don't worry about her."

"Breaking up?"

"Divorcing."

Tuttle knew Tetzel well enough to doubt his word, but the reporter didn't expend any energy trying to overcome Tuttle's doubt, and that argued that he was telling the truth.

"You figure she's just hiding out?"

"Something like that."

What was Chicago coming to when a half-hysterical claim that a young girl had been kidnapped met with such indifference? Tuttle drove over to Evanston and stopped by where Sonya lived.

"She's not in," a woman with enormous breasts said carefully.

"When do you expect her?"

"Are you a relative?"

"Police." Tuttle fumbled for his wallet but there was no need to go on.

"Look. I've told you everything I know. Talk with her parents."

"We don't like bothering you," Tuttle assured the stern woman. "But we have to take reports like this seriously."

The hawklike face softened. "I know, Officer. But how often do I have to tell the same story?"

Her story told him nothing except that someone was interested in Sonya, even if the Fox River Police were treating the missing girl as less than a priority item.

At the offices of EH the next day, Tuttle caught Craig Wilhelms in. "There's not much to report," Tuttle said, taking off the tweed hat and rubbing his brow.

"You a detective?"

Tuttle gave the man a little smile as if rewarding him for a shrewd guess. "When's the last time you saw her?"

"Me?"

Tuttle looked around to make sure there was no one else in the room. Who the hell did Wilhelms think he meant?

"Doesn't she ever come around here?"

"She's a student at Northwestern, Officer."

"I'm not a policeman."

At that point, Wilhelms should have told him to get the hell out of there. He should have been angry that Tuttle had let him think he was a cop.

"Who are you?"

Tuttle fished a card out of the top pocket of his jacket and handed it to Wilhelms, his mind revving as he did so. His hope in coming here was somehow to get EH as a client or, short of that, to get his hands on some of this outfit's ill-gotten gains.

"What's your interest in Sonya?"

"I'm not the kind of lawyer who solicits business," Tuttle said primly. He might crawl for it, trade his soul for it, but outright ask? No. A straight question asks for a straight denial.

"What kind are you?"

"The kind that might be of help to you."

"To me? I don't need help. Sonya needs help."

"Tell me what I can do."

But Wilhelms tipped back in his chair, seeming to lose interest in the subject. But maybe not.

"You wouldn't have heard of the Virginia Verona case. We kept that pretty quiet. Besides, it was Virginia who had been pestering Chris, so what would be her complaint? He kept her locked up for a week, she didn't know where she was. She couldn't even be sure it was Chris who came to her in the dark." Craig shook his head. "Weird."

Tuttle shook his head too. If only Virginia Verona had come to him for representation. But Wilhelms was right, he had never heard of it.

"Where did he lock her up?" It dawned on Tuttle that Craig might be telling him about Sonya.

Wilhelms got to his feet and gestured to Tuttle, indicating that he join him by the window. There he turned up the air conditioner and dropped his voice, making it very difficult for Tuttle to hear what he was saying. What the hell was this?

Wilhelms bisected his lips with his index finger. Using the wall, he wrote on the back of the card Tuttle had given him and handed it back.

"Get the hell out of here, Tuttle," he said, suddenly lowering the air conditioner and raising his voice.

On the back of the card he had written an address:
"8819 Highland. 6 tonight."

Wilhelms had opened the door of his office now and
he stood there and repeated in a loud voice, "Get the
hell out of here, Tuttle."

It was a somewhat confused Tuttle who hurried
through the outer office and out to his Toyota. Obviously Wilhelms did not want his secretary to know
they would be meeting. Either that or he was nuts. Or
a client. Or all three.

SEVEN

ROGER DOWLING was reading the *Summa Theologiae* in his study when he looked up to see Marie in the doorway, her face twisted in an expression whose significance he could not read.

"Christopher Bourke?" she said. "The one who was here the other day?"

"What's happened?"

"Did you know he had a daughter?"

"Yes."

"She's been kidnapped."

Marie managed to listen to WBBM all day while somehow at the same time following her quota of televised soaps. The continual radio news had carried the startling announcement by Janet Gray and Christopher Bourke that their daughter Sonya had been kidnapped.

For half a second he imagined Marie was pulling some awful trick on him, having guessed or somehow discovered the purpose of Chris Bourke's visit to the St. Hilary rectory. But that was absurd. She would never invent such a story. He put down his book and picked up his pipe. Meanwhile Marie turned on his radio and waited impatiently for it to warm up so she could get confirmation of the news announcement she had just heard in the kitchen. But of course the insatiable maw of the news was now devouring other events and happenings around the nation and the world, a man and a woman newscaster alternating items.

"Turn it off, Marie, and tell me what you heard."

"I already told you. They said the girl has been kidnapped."

She turned off the radio. The phone rang. Thank God he got it before Marie did.

"Roger?"

"Yes."

"Chris Bourke."

He looked at Marie, willing her out of the study, but she refused to look at him. Into the phone he said, "Yes, of course. What is it?"

"You haven't heard the news?"

"Yes, I have."

"Can you talk now?"

"I can listen."

Marie looked at him strangely. He waved at her, nodding toward the door. Her mouth opened in feigned surprise and she scooted out of the room.

"Close the door, Marie."

She closed the door. Hard.

"Chris, what's this about your daughter?"

"She's disappeared. She left a note. She says she's gone to join the convent."

"So she hasn't been kidnapped."

"That's a matter of interpretation, I suppose. Roger, could you find out where she is? I just couldn't tell Janet what Sonya has done."

"She thinks Sonya's been kidnapped?"

"That's easier on her than the truth would be."

"You're not serious."

"I am, Roger."

"Chris, if you know where she is, what do you want me to do?"

"But I don't know where she is. I have to know what convent she's in."

"Why?"

"Please help me, Roger."

Roger glanced at the *Summa*. Saint Thomas argued that a parent in hell could not wish his child to be there, so unnatural would that be. That a fallen-away priest could not wish his daughter to be in a convent seemed somehow the obverse of that, he was not sure why. Perhaps because what Chris Bourke was asking made so little sense, no more sense than the purpose of his visit to the rectory, asking Roger to speak to his daughter in the expectation that this would alter her desire to become a nun.

"If she left you a note, she has told you where she is. No doubt eventually you will hear from her again. In the meantime, does it really matter what convent she's in?"

"If she's in one."

"What exactly does the note say?"

"Roger, are you busy now?"

He had come to his study in the hope of having several hours for reading and smoking his pipe, combining the pleasures of tobacco and Thomas Aquinas, and it was difficult not to feel resentment at Chris's request. He had felt no impulse to shun the man when he came to the rectory. On the other hand, they had nothing in common except the priesthood Chris had tossed aside, and Marie could hardly be expected to welcome a second visit from one of the Church's most vocal local foes. If it hadn't been for Sonya and her incredible conversion he would have found a way to avoid telling Chris to come to the rectory. Maybe in the sinuous way of providence the daughter would prove to be the salvation of the parents.

"I'll buy you lunch."

Chris should realize that lunch away from the rectory was no treat for the pastor. "I'll be saying Mass at noon."

"I'll make a reservation for one."

"I may be held up."

"Roger, I can wait. I really do appreciate this."

For the rest of the morning, he fretted about Chris's call, annoying Marie by his unwillingness to oh and ah about the news of the kidnapping of the daughter of the infamous pair. Chris Bourke was having a bad effect on the disposition of Marie Murkin. The invitation to lunch had strained relations and Marie had gained Phil's agreement that it was a cause for scandal that the pastor of St. Hilary's had offered the hospitality of the rectory to an enemy of the Church. Now, knowing that the kidnapping was a cover story for the worse embarrassment of announcing that their daughter had run away to the convent, he must have seemed willfully incurious to Marie. She would have loved to sit down and have a good talk about this amazing turn of events.

"And to think he dropped in here out of the blue only days ago."

"Amazing."

"With all that money, I suppose the girl has been in danger all her life."

"I suppose."

His replies might annoy her but it would have been worse to encourage her belief that Sonya had been kidnapped. Eventually it would become clear that she hadn't been and doubtless then Marie would also learn that Roger Dowling had known the truth of the matter. Nonetheless it was tempting to trade a future annoyance that might somehow be avoided for present relief and enter into Marie's chatter about the missing Sonya Bourke.

"What kind of name is Sonya?" Marie asked.

"A first name."

She made a face. "Is there a Saint Sonya?"

"You can't canonize her just because she's missing."

"I mean who is she named after?"

All he could think of was Sonja Henie, an ice skater of long ago. Marie took a book from the shelf and seemed almost disappointed when she found Sonya among the names of the saints and thus an apt name to give someone in baptism. But then she looked up, her eyes wide.

"But what am I thinking of? I don't suppose the poor thing's ever been baptized."

That an unbaptized person had fallen into the hands
of desperate kidnappers added to the drama, of
course, and Marie chattered on about that while Roger
considered that it must be some kind of a crime to report a kidnapping that hadn't happened. It was an ir-
ritable pastor of St. Hilary's who went over to the
church to offer the noon Mass.

EIGHT

THERE WAS SOMETHING BOGUS about the way the two of them stood there in front of the camera, Janet's hand in Chris's, wearing twin shattered expressions as they told the world their daughter Sonya had been kidnapped. Cy and his wife had not been blessed with children, but he felt he knew a lot more about parental affection than either of the Bourkes. He felt nothing but contempt for these two. It wasn't simply that they had betrayed an institution and, presumably, their own youthful dreams and then had made a career out of ratting on the Church—Cy Horvath might feel glad when an ex-KGB agent spilled his guts in the West, but somehow you could never quite trust a man like that. But these two had made public what any decent person knew to be private. Why else are they called privates? Cy was deeply embarrassed by people like Janet and Chris who took it to be a mark of honesty to speak of every part of life as on the level of washing your hands. No one looking at the hulking lieutenant with his impassive Hungarian face would suspect that the heart of a poet beat within him, but when Cy made love to his wife, his heart sang and he could have wept with joy. How stupid for Chris and Janet to make eyes at one another and talk to a television audience about how good it had been last night.

If he felt this way about the two of them, Phil Keegan felt worse, and that, as Cy thought of it, was the trouble. As policemen they couldn't refuse to look into an alleged kidnapping even if everything they knew about the reporters of it inspired disbelief. In this case, not even Chief Robertson was after them to investigate the report about Sonya. Robertson had the vague notion that the whole thing was a publicity stunt and he was damned if he was going to act as shill for Chris Bourke. And then there was the chief's daughter Gloria.

Gloria, an overweight girl who had made her life more miserable by trying out for cheerleader, entering homecoming queen contests and auditioning for a leading role in play after play, always with unsuccess, had finally come into her own at the age of twenty-three when she began to listen to Chris and Janet on television. Hitherto, she had thought of her body as a stronghold to be protected from importunate men who were dying to get her into bed. Nothing in her experience with the opposite sex encouraged this view, but nonetheless she held it. Listening to Bourke she had seen the light, and in the first flush of liberation had offered herself to a delivery boy who chose that magic moment to arrive at the Robertson door. She was part of the studio audience as often as possible, she bought the tapes and videos, and soon her overheated mind led on to public escapades. She hung around bars in Old Town and twice had been arrested for prostitution, although there was never any question of money changing hands. The liberated Gloria simply wanted

to do it. Not even the dim light of bars and the lubri-
cation of booze made her attractive, and men she approached took offense. Poor Robertson had managed
to hush up her indiscretions, but of course he could
not keep it a secret from the department. It was one
occasion when Keegan had shown genuine sympathy
for the chief.

Reflecting on all this, Cy decided he must act for the
department and see what he could find out about
Sonya Bourke. And the thing that stuck in his mind
was that Bourke had been to visit Roger Dowling. Cy
distrusted intuition and had in Keegan a superior
whose distrust of hunches was stronger than his own.
Nonetheless, since he was acting out of character in
any case, pursuing a lead that both Keegan and Robertson had shelved, he began by stopping by the rectory and talking with Marie Murkin.

"Too bad about the Bourkes," he said, after she
had put him at the kitchen table with a cup of coffee
before him.

"Poor girl, you mean. And not just lately."

"He was here last week, wasn't he?"

Marie threw up her hands and lifted her eyes to
heaven. "I knew it. I told him. It would be a public
scandal."

"Captain Keegan told me. I don't think anyone else
knows."

"If only I could be sure of that."

"What was he like? How did he seem?"

"Slick as the devil."

"Why did he come?"

She dropped her head and looked at him over her glasses. "You're asking me to divulge parish business, private business?"

"I just wondered if it had something to do with the kidnapping, if maybe he was worried or had received a threat."

"I'm not at liberty to answer that, Lieutenant Horvath."

Marie said she was reluctant to talk, but she was even more reluctant to let him go. He had two pieces of rhubarb pie and another cup and a half of coffee, listening to Marie excoriate Christopher Bourke— "Father Bourke, and don't you forget it!"—and the diabolical message he spewed out on his television program.

"Enlightened Hedonism," she said. "Do you know what that means?"

"I get the general picture."

"He should be horse-whipped. Imagine letting them talk about such things on television."

"Father Dowling around?"

"No."

The following day, Cy drove out to St. Hilary's again. He parked by what had once been the parish school and watched the old folks frisking around on the playground. It was funny how life brought people full circle. Some of those senior citizens had attended St. Hilary's grade school and now here they were, retired, back at the same stand. He was about to drive off, thinking he was doing a little reverting himself, when he saw the stretch limo with the dark windows pull up at the rectory. He noted the license without realizing he was doing it. Moments later Roger Dowling came down the walk and got into the car.

Cy pulled out after the limo, putting in a call for a trace on the license number, feeling a bit like an idiot. But it was a day to play hunches, and when he was told the car was registered in the name of Christopher Bourke he kept on the tail until the limo pulled into a restaurant near O'Hare. Father Dowling got out first and then Chris Bourke and they went together into the restaurant.

NINE

TUTTLE PARKED THE TOYOTA in a handicapped spot a block from the address Craig Wilhelms had given him and sauntered casually up the street, portrait of a man strolling around his own neighborhood, if anyone should wonder. Except that no one lived in this part of Chicago, a sort of inner-city industrial park. The address he sought was a warehouse, a remodeled factory, with a list of occupants mounted in plastic on the wall. EH Inc. was among them. Tuttle relaxed, but kept right on going. There was no evidence that Craig Wilhelms had arrived. Ten to six. Tuttle whistled as he walked.

He had spent the time since leaving Wilhelms trying to keep a smile off his face, trying not to greet strangers, indulging in silent screams of ecstasy when he was sure no one was looking. There had been near misses in the past. He had come that close to El Dorado more than once, a lesser man would have resigned himself to defeat and mediocrity, but Tuttle was driven by an unspoken pact with his father. The paternal sacrifice was not to be made a mockery of by unrealized potential. And never had he felt closer to Big Casino than this evening.

Trying not to imagine what lay ahead, he had of course ticked off the possibilities. Would he be employed to negotiate with the kidnappers? The possibility exhilarated him. Bourke had already capitulated, it would be a matter of arranging the drop, getting a suitcaseful of money, skim off his retirement fund, get the girl and collect a handsome fee. If the money was regained, let the kidnappers explain the missing amount.

Or he would be retained to sue the city of Fox River for negligence; maybe they would file against Evanston as well. What kind of city would allow a young woman to be carried off in the light of day?

Or the note had finally arrived and legal advice was needed. "Get Tuttle," he imagined Chris Bourke saying, conveniently forgetting that he paid an uninvited call at EH and received an enigmatic response from Craig Wilhelms.

A more unsettling possibility occurred to him now, as he turned to walk back to the warehouse. Wilhelms had stashed the girl away and, having believed some of the malicious statements bruited about concerning Tuttle's ethics, imagined he could enlist the lawyer's help in shaking down his employers. Tuttle frowned. He would listen to the proposition, of course, if only to assuage his curiosity.

He jumped as a car pulled up behind him, coming to a stop just as its bumper brushed his leg. Craig jumped out of the car and, indicating Tuttle should follow, ran up the steps to the entrance of the warehouse. He had his key in the lock, turned and pushed open the door in one fluid motion. Tuttle followed him through. The heavy metal door squeaked shut behind him and he was in pitch-darkness.

"Wilhelms?"

"Come on."

"Where the hell are you?"

Tuttle lifted his hand but saw nothing. It was like losing a limb. What the hell was going on here? And then a rectangle of gray appeared in the inkiness and in it Craig Wilhelms was silhouetted. Another door. Tuttle started toward the gray, which swiftly shrank and disappeared to the clank of another door. Tuttle plunged forward and almost immediately banged into the closed door and began to beat on it.

"Hey, I didn't get through. I'm still here."

He continued to beat on the door with one hand while with the other he groped for the handle. There had to be a handle, Wilhelms had opened the door. He realized that he was yelling a sustained monotone yell. His hand found a keyhole but no handle.

How long did he stand there, pounding on the closed cold metal door, shouting, close to sobbing? He looked back over his shoulder and was almost surprised when his chin brushed his shoulder. He felt bodiless. The dark was, if possible, even darker than before. And it was cold, cold as an icebox. Thoughts of butchers caught in meat lockers when the door slammed shut came to him. He had never been so frightened in his life and the noise he was making added to his terror. He fell silent and a tomblike quiet enveloped him. He could hear his own heart beating, beating, like a story by Edgar Allan Poe.

Fear gave way to anger. He would kill Wilhelms when he got his hands on him, tear him limb from limb. He couldn't treat an officer of the court like this and get away with it. Tuttle began to sob.

The sound of his own sobbing filled him with self-pity and he imagined his father getting word of this on the other side, peering down and seeing his son imprisoned in the dark warehouse, helpless...

Stop it, he commanded himself. Stop it right now. And he did, as a smile broke out on his face. He felt it with both hands to make sure it was there. This was a practical joke. Any moment that door would be pulled open and what kind of idiot would he look like, standing there bawling his head off like a kid? He wiped his eyes with the brim of his tweed hat and clamped it on his head again. Backward? What difference did it make. He stood very still, getting ready to emerge blinking into the light, smiling like a good sport, old Tuttle could take a joke as well as anyone. Let's get on to the important stuff, the kidnapping.

Kidnapping. He himself was as kidnapped as anyone, led down the garden path by Craig Wilhelms and standing here in the dark of a warehouse, a dark that grew deeper if it altered at all. He listened, and sure enough, there was a sound. He put his ear against the door and listened and realized the sound was coming from behind him. Of course, the outer door. He turned around carefully, pressed his back against the door to get his bearings and then, hands out before him, moved back into the inky darkness, slowly, slowly, slowly, until his fingers came in contact with something. Not metal, concrete: the wall. With his left hand he found metal, the door, and edged toward it, listening.

A muffled voice came to him, someone calling. He got his ear against the door and his hand came down on a handle. He grasped it with both hands, pushed down on the thumb lever and tugged. Light and the blessed air of freedom rushed in at him and he flung himself outside and into someone's arms.

"Jesus, Tuttle, take it easy."

And there, as his eyes grew accustomed to the light, stood Peanuts Pianone, edging away in embarrassment from Tuttle's embrace. It was all Tuttle could do to let him go. In his vast relief he wanted to hug the air out of Peanuts.

"Whatcha come here for, Tuttle?"

It didn't occur to him to ask the same question of Peanuts. That his boon companion should have shown up at this critical moment seemed no stranger than the ordeal he had just been through. Tuttle looked wildly up and down the street.

"Where's the car that was parked here?"

Peanuts looked as if he were being accused of stealing it. "What car?"

"There was a car stopped right there minutes ago."

Minutes? His sense of time had deserted him. But the car had been real. He looked down at the calf of his leg against which the bumper of Craig Wilhelm's car had brushed. Was that a spot of dust?

"How'd you get here, Peanuts?"

Peanuts pointed and Tuttle saw the hood of a squad car just peeking out from between two buildings half a block away.

"Somebody had to drive that car away."

Peanuts shook his head and fished ignition keys from his pocket. "Not mine. I brought these with me."

"Come on."

Tuttle scurried to the corner of the building and followed the side wall to the back, Peanuts at his heels. They came to a large loading area, scarred wooden docks running along past large metal doors, all of which were shut. Tuttle handed himself up a ladder and moved along the dock. Craig Wilhelms must have come out this way. Hands on his hips, tweed hat lowered over his eyes, Tuttle surveyed the asphalt expanse. It was cracked, sprouting weeds, covered with old oil stains. Where the asphalt ended, dry weedy growth from last summer rose brittle and brown six feet high. Once in there, anyone would be out of sight and out of mind. He imagined the perfidious Wilhelms, having led him into the dark, barreling through the building, out of the sliding door and dashing across the asphalt to that stand of weeds.

But why? Disconcerting as it had been to be caught in the dark, the fact was, as he had discovered, he had not been locked in. All he had to do was retrace his steps and he was outside again.

Puzzled, he went around to the other side of the building again and pondered the disappearance of Wilhelms's car. There was no way the man could have exited by the door they both had entered. That would have lit up the anteroom and Tuttle himself would have followed.

Had Wilhelms been alone in the car? He realized he hadn't even noticed. If someone else had been in the car, all he had to do was slide behind the wheel and get the hell out of there.

"When you going to tell me what's going on?" Peanuts asked.

"It's very complicated."

"Yeah?"

"Let's go sit in the squad car."

They settled into the front seat, the radio crackling away, and Tuttle closed his eyes. Immediately he opened them. All his childhood fear of the dark was back. Peanuts sat behind the wheel, waiting patiently.

"Peanuts, what the hell brought you down here?"

"You."

"But how did you know..."

"I was following you."

"What the hell for?"

"I spotted your car and thought maybe we could go have a little Chinese."

"You just happened to see me drive by? Come on."

"It's true. How many Toyotas like yours are left?"

"If you were following me, you had to see the car."

"Of course I saw the car."

"Not mine! The one that was parked by the warehouse."

Peanuts had first parked near the Toyota and was about to get out and hail the pacing Tuttle when it occurred to him he might be interrupting something.

"Interrupting?"

"I thought maybe you were meeting some broad."

Tuttle was embarrassed. Women were a mystery to him. His mother had died when he was a child, and he had been raised by a doting father. It would have seemed disloyal to Tuttle senior if he had become interested in a girl, since it would have heralded his departure from the paternal roof. So he had put it off and put it off, and not reluctantly. What he knew about girls was not reassuring. He was used to frowns or whispered remarks, giggling. He didn't understand it. But he lived in the expectation that one day his true love would come along. In the meantime, he kept aloof from the female sex. The one or two times he had tuned into the EH broadcasts he had been astounded. That Peanuts should think he had made an assignation among these warehouses was a troubling thought. What did his old pal think of him?

But he was more interested in reviewing the events of the past hours. He told Peanuts of dropping by EH, just in case legal counsel was needed and the parties in question did not know how to proceed. He described Wilhelm's strange subterfuge with the air conditioner. and the scribbled message on his card.

"Show me."

"I left it in the Toyota. He told me to meet him down here. I came, he came, we went inside. It was totally dark, he kept going and I couldn't see where I was. So I decided to come back out again and there you were.''

"Why were you hollering in there?"

"I thought I was locked in."

"Aha," Peanuts said, looking sly, and Tuttle felt suddenly depressed. Why did he bother telling Peanuts these things? For therapeutic reasons, that's why. Just saying it all out loud helped, taming the awful time when he had felt locked into the dark warehouse. He had heard that outerspace was like that, dark as night. No astronaut career for Tuttle, that was for damned sure.

"Take me to the Toyota, would you, Peanuts?"

"You want Chinese?"

Peanuts Pianone liked Chinese food better than pasta and he counted on Tuttle's willingness to settle down with sweet-and-sour pork, fried rice of various kinds, egg rolls. Tuttle realized that he was ravenously hungry, but then he usually was. Peanuts had trouble getting the car in gear but eventually they emerged jerkily from between the buildings and Peanuts made a wide turn, bumped over a curb and started up the street.

"You're a hell of a driver, Peanuts."

"Thanks."

Tuttle let it go. Peanuts got moody when he realized he was being kidded. Fortunately that realization was rare.

At the Toyota, Tuttle got out.

"The Orient Express?" Peanuts called.

Tuttle nodded. There seemed to be something in his car, as if someone had thrown a coat into the back seat. He opened the door and saw the girl's legs first, exposed because her skirt had ridden up her hips. Her sightless eyes studied the back seat. She was dead. Tuttle knew who she was. Sonya Bourke.

TEN

PEANUTS PIANNONE had called in before bringing Tuttle downtown, and Keegan was sure the message had to be garbled, but then Agnes Lamb and her patrol companion checked it out and it was true. The dead body of a Caucasian female had been found in the back seat of the lawyer's Toyota. Cy Horvath went out to the scene and Peanuts brought Tuttle in. The little lawyer now sat despondently across from Keegan, head down, the brim of his hat concealing his face. Was he weeping?

"Tell me about it, Tuttle."

Tuttle tipped back his head and looked at Keegan. "Why would anyone do a thing like this to me, Captain? Do you know what a shock it is to find a dead body in your car?"

"It's never happened to me."

"Be grateful."

"Of course I don't go hanging around strange parts of town leaving my unlocked car where anyone could put anything in it. That's your story, isn't it?"

"It's not a story!"

"Someone set you up?"

"That's what I don't know. Why would they?"

"You still haven't told me what you were doing in that area."

Tuttle's eyes narrowed. "I was doing something for a client."

"Carting away a body?"

"Dammit, Keegan, cut it out. You've known me for how long?"

"You want a character reference from me, Tuttle, you're in trouble. Every time I run across you, you're up to something no lawyer ought to be up to."

"I resent that."

"So do I. What were you doing down there, Tuttle? Or do you want to be booked first?"

Tuttle held out for a few more minutes before swearing Keegan to a professional secrecy he himself was wanting. He began to talk. Keegan listened impassively, marveling at the shamelessness of the little lawyer. But then, if Tuttle didn't chase ambulances, where would he be?

"Craig Wilhelms made an appointment to meet you at that warehouse?"

"That's right."

The manner of his making the appointment was bizarre, but somehow it fit in with the kind of lawyer Tuttle was.

"Let me see the card."

"I don't have it."

"Why?"

"I left it in my car. I got it out to check the address and left it on the front seat. It was gone."

"Anyone else know Wilhelms meant to meet you at the warehouse?"

What Wilhelms's secretary could tell them was that her boss had ordered Tuttle from his office, giving him what used to be called the bum's rush. The secretary seemed to think Keegan was talking dirty when he used the phrase. Were all the employees at EH as horny as their employers? Imagine a decent girl working for such an outfit. But this redhead with the too-short skirt repeated the words she had heard Wilhelms use. It sounded like the kind of departure Tuttle must often make. The little lawyer practically wept when he swore Wilhelms had written that address on the back of his business card.

"His?"

"Mine."

"Yours?"

"How else would I have known where the warehouse is, Keegan. Tell me that."

"You're begging the question, Tuttle."

"I'm telling the truth."

"You better start lying then, because what you're saying isn't going to help."

"Yeah?" Tuttle rose. "I'm leaving, Captain. I've been the good citizen long enough. I've told you all I know and now I'm going."

But he did not move. He seemed to expect Keegan to order him to be seated or come around the desk and put the arm on him.

"Don't leave town."

"Don't leave town? You watching old movies or something?"

"Get the hell out of here, Tuttle."

The coroner, Jolson, put the girl's death twenty-four hours at most before the time of examination, so unless Tuttle had been carting her around in his car for a day or so, his story, unlikely as it was, was probably true. Besides, Peanuts claimed to be sure that when he had seen Tuttle in his car an hour before the discovery of the body, the back seat had been empty. How Peanuts could know that was a mystery, but Keegan had heard Peanuts on the stand. Once he said something he stuck with it, and Keegan knew he would stick with this.

Cy came in and described the scene where the body had been found. His description matched what Keegan remembered of the area. The girl was dead and it had seemed at first unclear how she had died. No marks on the throat, no bruises on the body. Then Jolson found the point of entry under the left breast, where the murder weapon had been thrust into her chest. The diameter suggested something like a needle.

"Or a hat pin," Jolson said, after looking over both shoulders. But he was still recording, so the guess was part of the record.

"Stabbed?"

"Right into the heart." Jolson jabbered on about the damage done that organ by the sharp-pointed instrument, but it was something that could only interest a pathologist.

"Whoever kidnapped her," Cy answered when Keegan asked aloud who would kill the girl. That was all. Keegan felt bad enough for neglecting the an-

nouncement the Bourkes had made about their
daughter. He felt even more guilty because it looked
as if he'd taken his cue from Robertson. The chief was
Keegan's cross, the idiot he had to pretend to take instructions from in his professional life. Robertson was
a political hack, the beneficiary of the one-party pol-
itics of Fox River. Normally, Keegan assumed that the
opposite of anything Robertson said was where the
truth lay, but in this case he had been genuinely moved
by what the chief had been put through by his overweight daughter. The kid might have gone bad without the help of Chris Bourke and his so-to-speak wife,
but the fact was that the duo had aided and abetted
Gloria's descent to a life on the street. If Gloria did it
for money they could run her in, but in the present
climate of the country, how could you even speak dis-
approvingly of a woman who was promiscuous in
bars, let alone arrest her? The last prostitute arrested
in Fox River had used freedom of speech as a defense
and was still appealing on that basis. Keegan, as the
father of two daughters he seldom saw, since that required taking time off from work and traveling across
the country, felt a profound sympathy for the chief
and, like Robertson, half-hoped the Bourkes were finally getting theirs. But what he had actually assumed was that it was one more publicity stunt on the
part of the ex-nun and former priest. Keegan was determined not to collude with them in whatever fraud-
ulent sacrilege they were now embarked upon.

But now the daughter had shown up dead. Keegan
was grateful Cy did not remind him of his delin-
quency, but then Cy would never do a thing like that.

"Roger Dowling met with Bourke a few days ago," Cy said.

"The guy just dropped by at the rectory. What was Roger supposed to do?"

"This was another meeting, at the Wattle Inn near O'Hare."

"How would you know a thing like that?"

Cy told Keegan about being parked by the playground at St. Hilary's watching the retired parishioners entertain themselves, when the stretch limo pulled up in front of the rectory and Father Dowling got in.

"You followed it?"

"I checked out the license and when I heard it was Bourke, I wondered if it could possibly have anything to do with the alleged kidnapping."

"Alleged?"

Of course Cy was right. The fact that the girl was dead didn't prove she'd been kidnapped. Keegan would have felt a lot better if he didn't think Cy was trying to make him look better than he deserved.

"There was never a note."

"You checked with the parents?"

"I mean they never reported any demands."

"Cy, the nut practically invited the kidnapper to take him for all he had. That's what made me doubt it was a legitimate snatch. I'm not excusing myself."

Cy ignored it. "That's why I thought he might have made a deal and wanted Dowling along as a witness."

"But that wasn't it?"

"They just had lunch."

"They could have been talking about a note, a phone call, something."

"That's right."

But after they ate, Bourke drove Roger back to the rectory and that was that. Well, not quite. Cy had followed Bourke.

It made a cop's life sound like fun and games, but Keegan was glad Cy had done what he'd done. The lieutenant's report made the sequence sound perfectly rational, as if he was just out there doing what he'd been told to do. The question was, did the lunch mean anything? Whether it did or not, Roger Dowling was not going to let Keegan in on private conversations.

"Where did Bourke go?"

Cy rolled from one haunch to the other. "He was dropped off at a station in Glenview and took the train to Niles."

"You followed him?"

"I went back for the car."

"Where did he go?"

Cy read the address and Keegan waited. "It's the apartment of a woman named Maud Kaiser. She wasn't home, but her niece was there."

"Her niece?"

"Loraine Howells, a producer at EH studios."

"And?"

"He was there for an hour and twenty minutes. He left alone, took the train several stops, and caught a cab home."

"What do you think?"

"What d'you think."

Hanky-panky at a time when his daughter was allegedly kidnapped and he and his wife distraught enough to call a press conference?

"At which he invited the kidnappers to take him for all they wanted."

"How long has he been seeing Loraine Howells?"

"That's why I came to you. How much do we want to know about Chris Bourke?"

"Everything."

"Should I put Agnes on it?"

"Good." Agnes Lamb, who had been hired as a parlay, meant to be a token woman as well as a token black, two for the price of one, turned out to be one of the best detectives in the department. Keegan would have liked to claim this was due to his tutelage, as Cy Horvath had been schooled by him, but whatever she had learned from him had been indirectly and negatively. For a year he gave her a rough time and even after he recognized her talent, it took a while before he admitted it. He didn't like the idea of women cops, and as for blacks, most of his experience with them had been in his role of arresting officer. Now Keegan greatly admired Agnes, and he wasn't above letting her know it from time to time. As a God-fearing Baptist, she would be ideal to look into Chris Bourke and Janet Gray.

"What am I looking for?" Agnes asked.

"I wish I knew. I thought the kidnapping announcement was a phony. Maybe it was and maybe it wasn't. In any case the girl's dead. Bourke is goofing off with a television producer who works for him. Loraine Howells. Tuttle claims he was lured into a warehouse area by Craig Wilhelms. The body was found in his car. Tuttle's an ass and witnesses deny his story, but why would he tell it? Set it up and go full tilt, and I want daily reports.''

"What about Father Dowling?"

"What about him?"

"Cy says Dowling had lunch with Bourke after the kidnapping announcement and the day before the body was found."

"I'll take care of Dowling."

"Why?"

Keegan bristled. "For one thing, he's an old friend. I know him. He'll talk to me."

"What's another?"

"Another what?"

"Another reason why Roger Dowling isn't part of my assignment."

Keegan glared at her. "Okay, he is. I'll be acting for you when I talk with him."

Agnes revealed her glistening smile in slow motion. "Can I have Peanuts as well?"

"Pianone!"

"He's got a head start with Tuttle. Besides, he hates my guts."

"Don't make that a qualification for working with you."

"I don't. *You're* helping me, aren't you?"

ELEVEN

MARIE MURKIN did not like to tell God His business, tempting as that often was, but the tragedy of Sonya Bourke sent the housekeeper over to the church to say a rosary on her knees before the Blessed Sacrament. As she prayed, she acknowledged the limitations of her understanding and the impurity of her motives. It seemed presumptuous to congratulate God, but that's pretty much what Marie did. That the death of a young woman scarcely more than a girl was involved was tolerable only because God was in charge. Sooner or later He will take everyone to Himself and when you think of a person going to heaven sooner rather than later, the sadness of loss is diminished.

Marie prayed for the repose of Sonya Bourke's soul and asked forgiveness for her own first reaction to the unfolding events. Imagine the way she had behaved the day Christopher Bourke showed up at the rectory. Not that it wasn't understandable, mind, a man who had made a living saying awful things about the Church and his own priesthood brazenly standing on the doorstep of the St. Hilary rectory. Was she supposed to welcome him with open arms?

But she shook away such distractions and concentrated on her beads. When she went back to the rectory, she found Father Dowling standing on the back porch, smoking his pipe. Marie wouldn't admit it even to herself but she loved the smell of tobacco. She felt she ought to nag the pastor into quitting, but it seemed so small a thing. Her thoughts were not so irenic that night when Phil Keegan arrived and the two men settled in the study before the television, Captain Keegan smoking a cigar, Father Dowling smoking his pipe. Marie stood in the doorway waving her hand before her face.

"Anything I can get you before I go upstairs? Besides gas masks?"

"I'd like another beer," Phil said.

"You haven't finished that one."

"You're the one who volunteered."

When she returned with the beer, they were talking about the Bourke girl.

"Is it true she was murdered?" Marie asked Phil Keegan.

"With a narrow sharp instrument. Answer me a question, Marie. Do you have a hat pin?"

"A hat pin!"

"Then you don't."

"I haven't even seen a hat pin in years."

"Where would you go if you wanted one?"

"What store? No store carries such a thing anymore."

"A garage sale?" Father Dowling asked.

"Oh, you can get anything at a garage sale." Marie stepped back, putting it together. "You think she was killed with a hat pin?"

"The coroner does. Something like it, anyway."

"For heaven's sake." Such a weapon conjured up the image of an irate old lady, and Marie wasn't so sure she wanted the parents off the hook so easily.

"Well, if you don't have a hat pin, I guess that clears you, Marie."

"Clears me?"

"Father Dowling tells me you were saying some fierce things about the Bourke family."

"Family! You call that a family? Why, those two—" She stopped, unsure she could control her anger.

"I see what Roger meant," Phil Keegan said, studying her with narrowed eyes.

Marie looked back and forth between the two men. There were times when she didn't mind being teased, up to a point, but the spectacle of two grown men sitting there making light of a dreadful thing like a murder was too much. She made a straight line of her mouth, lifted and dropped her shoulders, turned on her heel and marched down the hall to her kitchen.

At the table, still seething, she poured the last cup of tea of the day, trying to ignore the steady rumble of male voices coming from the study. She shouldn't let them upset her so, but she had no defense against being teased. When she was a girl, Ruth, her older sister, had been a relentless teaser, and what was worse, she always enlisted her friends, male and female, in the effort. It wasn't malicious, Marie was sure, just a bad habit. The pastor of St. Hilary's had the same tendency, and when Phil Keegan was in the house, the two of them would get going on her. Laugh it off, that was the only defense, she knew that, but only seldom could she summon the strength to employ this weapon. Too often, like now, she got all het up and had to flee.

She pushed away her cup of tea, took another bottle of beer from the refrigerator, and marched back to the study. She collected the empties, poured half the new bottle into Phil's glass, and looked inquiringly at the pastor.

"You're all right?"

"Thanks, Marie."

"I thought you were going to bed," Phil Keegan said, but he wasn't teasing.

"I'd sleep a lot better if I knew what you've learned about the Bourke girl."

"She'd been thinking of entering the convent," Father Dowling said.

Phil Keegan, who had been about to say something, swung around and faced the pastor.

"You're not serious."

"It's why Chris Bourke came here. He wanted me to talk with her. There's no reason to keep it confidential now."

"A convent!" Marie pulled up a straight-backed chair and sat. If Father Dowling was teasing he would have Phil Keegan to deal with as well as herself. But clearly he was serious. Marie listened with rapt attention. Thank God she had swallowed her pride and returned to the study. It was so eerie to think that the daughter of such a union, raised the way that girl had been raised, whose parents had actually said they would have gotten an abortion if it had been legal at the time Janet Gray was pregnant with Sonya, should nonetheless find herself drawn to the ideal her mother had rejected. It must have come like a warning voice from above, their daughter talking about a vocation when the two of them had spent years mocking all talk of consecrating oneself to Christ. Janet Gray had been particularly offensive discussing the tradition of speaking of religious women as brides of Christ.

Marie had snapped off the television to rid herself of that smirking face and suggestive tone of voice. Glory be to God, had the woman no fear of divine retribution? Divine retribution had come in a strange way. They might reject the Church and the notion of a life given to God, but Sonya had heard the call.

"What did he expect you to do, Roger?"

"He didn't think she had a clear idea of what entering the convent meant."

"He expected you to talk her out of it?"

"Just talk to her. He knew I wouldn't talk her out of it. All he asked was that someone lay it out for her."

"He was reconciled to it?"

"Oh, I wouldn't say that."

Marie said, "I'm sure they would have stopped at nothing to prevent it."

Keegan looked at her. "Nothing?"

"What fools it would make them look."

"So they killed her?"

"I didn't say that!"

"I did. It's a thought worth pursuing."

"Now I'm sorry I told you," Roger Dowling said. "You mustn't let the press get hold of that."

"To hell with the press. It does help a bit to have a motive. The girl had not been harmed in any way, she hadn't been robbed. She had been stabbed with—let's say a hat pin. Why? Marie's right. Chris Bourke and Janet Gray had a motive."

Later, upstairs in her apartment, reached by her private stairway in the back of the house, Marie continued to tingle with Father Dowling's revelation. The daughter of two television merchants of sexuality enters the convent. Earlier that day in church, Marie had marveled at the mysteriousness of God's ways. At the time she'd had no idea how mysterious His ways really had been.

TWELVE

KATIE POWELL AND SONYA had watched Sonya's parents announce that their daughter was missing, kidnapped, had heard them say they would do anything to get news of her and to have her safely home. The two girls were in the basement rec room of the Powell family home in Waukegan. Katie's parents were in Sarasota still, and the house provided just the sort of place Sonya needed to think her way out of the crazy idea she had of entering the convent.

"I wouldn't have gotten the crazy idea if it hadn't been for you."

"Me?"

"Katie, have you any idea how different your outlook is?"

"What are you talking about?"

Sonya ticked off the points on the fingers of her hand. Katie went to Mass every Sunday, sometimes during the week. Sonya must have meant holy days of obligation. She was not, in the phrase, sexually active, nor did she particularly care for people who were. She spoke of life as if it possessed a clear meaning that must be the measure of what she did. And she smoked.

"What's smoking got to do with it?"

"You're not afraid of dying."

"Don't kid yourself. Besides, I've tried to quit. And please don't blame me for this idea of sealing yourself in a convent for the rest of your life. I have never in my whole life ever been attracted by any such thing."

"But you could have been. It would fit in with everything else."

It was amazing how one person could appear to another, even to someone you thought you knew better. Katie did not recognize herself in the description Sonya gave, making her sound like a religious nut, someone so good she made you sick. Go to Mass? Catholics go to Mass, it was part of what it meant. As for the other stuff, Katie didn't really believe all the stories of kids doing it all the time.

"Think of our friends," she said.

"Cassie?" asked Sonya.

"Not Cassie. Barb."

"Barb and Leonard."

"What about Barb and Leonard?"

"That's another thing. You're naive."

"Thanks a lot."

"And you say your prayers every day."

It was a habit, a morning offering when she woke, the Angelus around midday, on her knees beside her bed at night. Did Sonya think you grew out of such habits?

"Didn't you say that's what they call the dress nuns wear, habits?"

"Sonya, forget about nuns. Nuns are Catholics."

"I'll join."

"So you can dress up?"

That hadn't been fair. Katie apologized. It became inescapable that Sonya already thought of herself as a Catholic. Katie had never known anyone who entered a convent. The few nuns who taught at the high school she had attended looked just like anyone else. Well, not like anyone else. They just didn't know how to dress. They should have kept their habits. Twenty-five-year-old photographs in the school corridors featured nuns in truly beautiful habits. Long white robes, black veils, bright scrubbed faces looking at once wise and innocent. Had she ever imagined herself a nun? It would have been like imagining oneself born twenty-five years before.

The first time Sonya said she would like to live that kind of live, in a convent, not teaching high school, not doing anything she might do otherwise, but secluded, away, Katie had thought the obvious thing.

"There are lots of easier ways to hurt your parents."

Imagine what a sensation it could create. Katie had been hesitant when Cassie suggested they include Sonya Bourke as the third partner in the rental of the apartment. At first she hadn't made the connection, but Cassie told her, in whispers, and Katie imagined what her folks would say.

"She's not at all what you'd think," Cassie said.

"How do you know what I think?"

"What anyone would think. Did you ever listen to her parents' program?"

Katie had, openmouthed, shocked. She'd heard of channels, closed to all but paying customers, that showed unbelievable things, but EH was beamed on an open channel and here were these two beautiful if aging people talking about the importance of sexual satisfaction as if it were some kind of healthful exercise. The program did not prepare her for Sonya who, as Cassie had assured her, was not at all what she would have thought. It was Cassie who shocked her when she decided to move in with a dreadful boy with long greasy hair and eyes that seemed focused on something several galaxies away.

"But, Cassie, the rent."

"I talked to Sonya."

"What's that supposed to mean?"

"Ask her."

Sonya offered to pay two-thirds of the rent until they found someone to replace Cassie.

"I can't let you do that."

"Please. It doesn't matter that much to me, the money. I don't want to lose this place."

On that basis they really hadn't needed a third, and within a month they stopped looking. Sonya was a delight to live with. She didn't need music on full-blast, as Cassie did, and she seemed genuinely interested in study.

It started when Sonya said she had been downtown and looked into a church and it felt like going home. Katie was embarrassed. She had been born Catholic, it was just what she was. She believed it, she practiced it, but with the realization that zillions of people weren't Catholic and no doubt God knew how to get through to them. She wasn't interested in persuading anyone to become a Catholic. It would be like changing nationalities.

"I'll come with you," Sonya said one Sunday morning, looking out the door of her room.

"It starts at nine."

"I'm nearly ready."

The trouble with having a non-Catholic beside you at Mass was you kept wondering what it all looked like to them. The priest was an old man with a thin, muscular neck supporting a head that looked like a tennis ball. The PA system was remote and he didn't know how to use it, so his voice faded away, then came roaring back. The sermon was pretty bad. Sonya loved it. She found it all strange and mysterious.

"I thought it was in Latin."

"Not for years."

"Do you remember it?"

"No."

Sonya heard of a church where there was a Latin Mass once a week and urged Katie to go with her. There were three priests and incense and chant and that was stranger than the Latin.

"I guess I like the English better."

"I thought you'd want to try the Orthodox next."

"What's that like?"

"I'm kidding."

"I only know one prayer." And Sonya recited it. "Now I lay me down to sleep, I pray to God my soul to keep. If I should die before I wake, I pray to God my soul to take."

Talk of the convent came next and Katie began to think Sonya meant it.

"What do your folks think?"

"What do you know of my folks?"

"Tell me."

How awful it must have been to be raised like that, a studio prop when she was a child, the unwitting star of home movies shown on television.

"Being bathed?"

"Well, in the tub."

"What was the point?"

"That fascination with sex begins at birth. They really believe that. It's all they have left to believe. People think it's just a way to make money, but they could have made money doing a talk show, some other kind of show. At least I think so. But they never thought of it. It was their substitute for religion. All my life I've heard about sex, sex, sex. I got so sick of the word. Of course they assumed that I was sexually active."

"Have you ever . . ."

"Never."

Katie believed her as only one virgin can believe another. Katie herself looked forward to marriage and a husband and, yes, sex, but she could wait. For Sonya the convent seemed to be a refuge, a place away from the pursuit of pleasure, but that was less and less it.

"Prayer. Silence. Living only for God."

Katie nodded, embarrassed. She said her prayers but she had never thought of it as a treat. Sonya made it sound like the most satisfying activity in the world.

She began to believe Sonya really did belong in the convent.

And then Sonya told her parents and the whole picture changed.

"What did they say?"

"My mother would rather see me dead. Of course she has already told the world she wished she'd had an abortion when she was expecting me."

"They can't very well stop you."

Sonya didn't seem so sure. One day she phoned and said she didn't want to come home, so Katie went to the campus and drove into a parking garage where Sonya waited. They drove by a circuitous route to Waukegan. Katie got a kick out of all the hide-and-seek but she didn't really believe Sonya was in danger until, in the rec room of her parents' home, they saw Sonya's parents announce that she had been kidnapped.

"Now whatever happens to me is covered," Sonya said.

Katie left her there, they both agreed it was safer, and safer still if no one was told.

The first day she called Sonya from a pay phone and everything was all right.

"I feel like a thief eating all this food."

"Don't be silly."

"What if your parents walked in?"

"They're in Florida."

"Or a neighbor wonders who's in the house?"

"They'll think it's me."

The second day, the phone wasn't answered. Katie tried it again and again. Finally she drove to Waukegan, opened the garage door with remote control and closed it behind her after driving in. The house was quiet in the way only an empty house is quiet.

"Sonya?"

She went slowly up the stairs, calling Sonya's name, knowing she was not there. The bed in which she'd slept was made. There was no sign that she had been there. No indication when or why or how she had left. It seemed clear to Katie that Sonya's parents had found her and taken her away.

Now, two days after the finding of Sonya's body, she was once more in Waukegan, in hiding herself, although she did not know from what.

THIRTEEN

"I'M SURPRISED they didn't ask you to preside," Marie sniffed, when the news of the cremation of the body of Sonya Bourke came on WBBM.

Roger Dowling said nothing. The cremation had occurred as quickly as possible after the body was released to the parents, as if these dreadful days could be reduced to ashes and scattered to the wind. And indeed it might have been the last attention paid to the matter. In the days that followed, if it hadn't been for Phil Keegan, the pastor of St. Hilary's would have assumed that the world had entirely lost interest in poor Sonya Bourke. Not that Phil had much to tell. In fact, he came to ask questions.

"You had lunch with Chris Bourke the day after he announced his daughter was missing."

"I don't remember having told you that."

"You didn't."

Roger waited. He had the uncomfortable feeling most people must have when questioned by Phil. The only defense was to outwait the questioner.

"Cy happened to see you there."

"Happened to? It didn't seem the kind of place he'd enjoy."

"He followed you."

"Was I being watched?"

"No."

"You had assigned me police protection?"

"It was Bourke's stretch limousine he was following. Then you got out."

ROGER HAD FELT ODD riding in the plush limousine, with facing leather seats, a bar, television, and other perks that only the longest trip would justify. Chris poured himself a diet drink when Roger declined. The car had come to a stop at an intersection, and Roger realized that a man on the walk looking with disgust at the limo could not see through the windows. Thank God.

"McDivvit's here," Marie had cried, when the car pulled up in front of the rectory.

She meant the funeral director. Looking out the window, Roger thought for a moment she might be right, but he was waiting for Chris and he realized that the ostentatious car must be his. How had he arrived when he first came to the rectory?

"Who is it?" Marie asked, stepping aside so he could open the door.

"A friend from the seminary."

Her puzzled look gave way to horrified comprehension as he went outside. Poor Marie. But how did she think he felt, being called for like Cinderella going to the ball?

Chris made small talk on the way to the restaurant, wanting to reminisce about Quigley and Mundelein. Roger expected this from laicized priests, they couldn't keep a conversation away from their clerical past when they were with someone who would understand, but it was a surprise when Chris Bourke said, "Remember Slalom?"

Skorski had taught Old Testament and Hebrew to those who volunteered for it and the combination of that and the "ski" at the end of his name seemed to be the basis for the nickname, though by the time Roger and Chris came on the scene its origin was lost in the mists of time, sort of like the religious practices Slalom suggested were the analogues and antecedents of Jewish and Christian rites.

"Vividly."

"How many of us took Hebrew?"

Roger had the sudden image of a classroom, chalk dust hanging in a mote of light that seemed to warm the slate blackboard it lay upon. Through the open window came the sounds of freedom, other seminarians at their recreation, and the smell of spring. Slalom turned from the board and peered with nearsighted hope at his handful of students.

"I got it all backward."

"Ho ho," they had laughed.

"What about Slalom?"

"Nothing. I think of him from time to time. It never occurred to me then that he was brilliant, but he was. It wasn't simply that he knew a difficult language, he was far ahead of his time as a biblicist."

Not what Roger would have thought of as high praise. Slalom had indeed preceded the flood of biblical debunkers and demythologizers in the Church, and more than one seminarian came away from his class wondering why the Church made such a fuss over what amounted to folklore. Slalom ended his days in an apartment in Sarasota, reading John D. Mac-Donald mysteries and lamenting the Vatican II Declaration on Revelation for reasons Roger had never understood.

"It didn't go far enough," Chris suggested.

"How far is far enough?"

Chris raised his brows. "About where I've gotten."

It seemed libelous to suggest that Slalom had longed to kick aside the traces in the way Chris had. But Roger was to learn that Chris liked to imagine that he had simply carried to their logical conclusion premises held by his old professors. It was a bit like hearing a homosexual claim that anyone interesting was one of the group.

"Sonya's run away," Chris said at the Wattle Inn when his drink had arrived and the time for serious talk had come.

"Away from what?"

"She's not at her apartment in Evanston. Her roommate called to tell me she was gone. She sent this." He took out a folded piece of paper that apparently had been torn from a school notebook. It had the look of having been much read.

Dear Mom and Dad,

This is to let you know that I am going to try to get into a convent. This is not a drill. You should be able to remember what it's like to want to do what I'm doing. I'm counting on that. I know I used to threaten to do something like this but please don't think this is some way to hurt or embarrass you. It is what God wants me to do.

Love, Sonya

Chris was staring abjectly at him when Roger looked up from reading the note.

"Well?"

"It was good of her to let you know."

Chris sat back. "Good of her." He shook his head. "But you don't know what it's like having children, do you?"

"What is it like?"

"Roger, you must have heard or read about the tensions in the nuclear family. It's all true. All of it. We create a special little hell for ourselves once we let nature call the tune, and of course she does every time a wife gets pregnant. From that moment the relationship changes, it gets out of control, deep irrational forces come into play."

It was Roger's turn to sit back. "Did you ask me to lunch in order to tell me bunk like that?"

Chris laughed. "No." His expression became tragic again. "Help me, Roger. For God's sake. Nobody's going into convents anymore. I don't want her to waste even a year or two on that sort of..." He stopped.

"Chris, you keep coming to the wrong person. There isn't any right person, for that matter. It's true that I don't know what it's like to have children. But I can remember when I first realized I had a vocation."

"A vocation. Roger, you chose to be a priest, that's all."

"And so did you."

"That's right. But I got over it. It has marked me for life nonetheless. What would my life have been like if I'd escaped the whole notion of the priesthood?"

They ordered salmon but Roger found it difficult to enjoy it. It had the vague taste of a bribe but there was no way he, or anyone else, could do what Chris wanted done.

"Find out where she is, Roger. That's all I ask. You can do it. Just tell me what convent she's in."

"And what will you do then?"

"I just have to know."

He was lying. All too easily Roger could imagine him descending on the convent with court orders, wild claims that his daughter had been brainwashed. Everything in Chris's career since he left the priesthood pointed in such a direction. Certainly it would be a way to neutralize the negative effect of such news on his television show. Did he really care at all about his daughter? Roger left Chris that day with the distinct feeling that he had been given a glimpse of what was called damage control.

IT WAS IMPOSSIBLE to think that Chris would have had any premonition that his daughter would be found in the back seat of a car parked in a warehouse district.

"Tuttle's car!"

"We're not making much of that, Roger. The poor son of a gun has enough trouble making a living without that."

"Had his car been stolen?"

"No."

"What was he doing in that part of town?"

"That's the interesting part."

That Craig Wilhelms claimed and his secretary confirmed that he had thrown Tuttle out of his office at EH Productions did not seem to disturb Phil's interest in Tuttle's account.

"You think Wilhelms did lure him to the warehouse so someone could put the body in his car?"

"Why would Tuttle make up such a story? It makes him look like a damn fool and he knows it. And Pianone saw him come out of the warehouse and they were together for five or ten minutes before Peanuts drove Tuttle to where he had parked his car and they discovered the body. Peanuts says the body wasn't in the back seat earlier."

"Where was her father when the coroner thinks death occurred?"

"Chris? Oh, he's covered."

"How so?"

"He says he was with you."

"Our lunch?"

"The only problem with that, it was over too soon."

Roger Dowling breathed a little prayer of relief. What would Marie say if the pastor of St. Hilary's turned out to be the alibi of an apostate like Chris

Bourke, no matter that the man had just lost his only daughter by a violent death?

"Where did he go after our lunch?"

Phil glanced toward the door, then leaned toward Roger and whispered, "To visit a woman."

"Well, well."

"Only he doesn't know that we know that."

"But he has an alibi?"

"You don't have to rub it in."

Phil made no mention of Katie Powell, although Roger already knew from the girl that she had been questioned by Agnes Lamb. Katie had come to him direct from the cremation, her eyes red from crying.

"Sonya told me her father talked with you."

"Tell me about her."

"Father, what an awful thing that is, a cremation. I had never seen one before."

"There is no painless way of dealing with the dead."

"But this is pagan. It's like getting rid of trash. Why does the EPA permit it?"

"EPA?"

"The Environmental Protection Agency."

Roger understood. The Church now permitted cremation but he always counseled against it. The Church's opposition had been due to the fact that cremation was regarded by its proponents as a rejection of all the mumbo jumbo Christians associated with death, particularly the hope of resurrection. Well, a buried body was very soon as unlikely-looking a candidate for rising again as an urnful of dust, but there was the note Katie had detected, a desire to rid oneself of the deceased, to turn the dead into memories only.

"Did Sonya ever mention to you what convent she wanted to join?"

"She seemed to think I'd know all about convents. The only nuns I ever knew taught in my high school and there were only three of them."

FOURTEEN

MAUD KAISER played duplicate bridge three afternoons a week, budgeted twenty-five dollars a week for Lotto, went to the track in season, and swore she had never won a thing in her life. Whenever she said that, the image of her late husband Merle would come unbidden to mind. Merle had been the biggest loser of all, in life, but he had left this Vale of Tears spectacularly, going down in flames in the only airplane flight he'd ever taken. To Maud's amazement, Merle had bought an enormous amount of insurance before boarding the plane, as if he'd had a premonition. A speculative, otherworldly look came into Maud's eyes when she said this, although she was convinced that if Merle had thought he was heading for the last roundup and could clean up on insurance in the process, he would have gotten safely to Denver and the reunion of his World War II army platoon. Like herself, Merle had the gift of not winning. But that one bet he had made, on his life, had put Maud on Easy Street. Thanks to Merle she was never to know want again, never to have to work. Her life would be complete if she could persuade her niece Loraine to move in with her. Rent-free. It wasn't just that she was goodhearted (although where, when you stopped to think of it, was Loraine going to get a deal like that?) but at seventy-three it just made sense to have a young person around. In case. Maud left the thought incomplete. She was able to grasp that everyone else was mortal, doomed to die, but she did not like to apply this thought to herself.

"We'd just get in one another's way," Loraine would say, when Maud brought it up.

"How much are you paying for that apartment?"

"Maud, I wouldn't live anywhere without paying my way."

"So pay me, if you have to. I'll bank it and it will be that much more going to you, in case..."

"Any money you leave will go to Barney."

"Barney! I'd rather give it to the poor."

"That's what I said."

Maud made a face. She didn't like others criticizing her son, no matter how much she did it herself, no matter that Loraine had reasons of her own. Merle had been a dogged and dutiful provider, never bringing home much, but always enough, enough to buy this narrow brick house in what had once been an almost fashionable neighborhood on the South Side, enough to keep her and the boy fed and clothed, and Barney in school besides. School. Once she had rejoiced at Barney's interest in learning. He had enrolled at Roosevelt University and gone there year after year, until Maud and Merle began to wonder how much longer he intended to go to school. They learned that the classes Barney had been taking formed to pattern; he had fulfilled the requirements for no major but was within a course or two of a sufficiency of credits in philosophy, psychology, history, English, and sociology. He had an insatiable love of learning. And bad grades. His interest in a course waned by the time the final examination came around and invariably he did poorly, if indeed he took the examination at all. His approach to education was, he told Merle and Maud, "non-utilitarian." They came to understand that he meant he never intended to complete his studies and go on to gainful employment. He haunted used-book stores, spending whole days in Powell's warehouse on State Street, buying with great judiciousness, picking up an occasional rare book or curiosity. Merle had paged through a copy of a French work by a poet named Villon, illustrated with filthy watercolors, and threatened to throw it and Barney out of the house.

"That one volume is worth five hundred dollars," Barney said.

"Bullshit."

Barney produced a catalog and directed Merle's attention to an entry.

"I never thought a dirty book was worth that much."

"It's not dirty."

Merle angrily opened the book and pointed. "What would you call that?"

Barney said something in what he said was French and Maud didn't like that at all. What was becoming of the boy? It took a while to admit that her own son was, well, strange. Loraine complained that he was following her about. She would turn around and there he was. He didn't bother her, it was just that he was always *there*. Maud told herself that Barney was just being protective. Working for Christopher Bourke did seem a vulnerable position for a young woman as attractive as Loraine.

"She's nuts," Barney said, when Maud brought it up.

"Barney, she sees you."

"It must be her conscience."

He was lying. He was no better at it than his father. Did he keep on haunting Loraine? Loraine didn't bring it up anymore, so maybe not, but Barney became impossible to live with. Maud threatened to make him leave the house, quoting the cowardly Merle as authority. After Merle's death, Maud did throw Barney out. Well, she packed up his things, put them on the porch, had the locks changed and refused to answer when he leaned on the bell.

"At least call me a taxi," he shouted through the locked door.

"A taxi?"

"How'm I gonna carry this stuff otherwise?"

She called him a cab. It came and Barney lugged his belongings down to it and got into the back seat with the wooden box containing his precious books on his lap. Maud watched dry-eyed as the taxi went up the street and out of view.

There were times—when Loraine just smiled and shook her head as Maud told her how nice it would be if she moved in with her—that Maud regretted locking Barney out. He wasn't much of a companion, but

he was better than nothing. Not that she had given up
on Loraine. Sooner or later, the girl would have to see
the light and move in. Maud had given her a key to the
house.

"Why do I need a key?"

"In case you come when I'm not home. I play
bridge three afternoons a week."

"I don't believe it."

Maud ticked off the days and places proudly. In part
she wanted Loraine to get a glimpse of what the good
life was like; in part she wanted to remind herself how
nice things were for her. Loraine took the key, dropping it in her purse.

"It seems silly, but why not?"

When Mrs. Zinser next door asked who the young
woman was who was in the house from time to time,
Maud knew that her niece was taking the bait. It didn't
bother her a bit to think of Loraine in the house when
she was out. If she couldn't trust her only brother's
only child, whom could she trust? There was nothing
around to shock the girl, now that Barney's dirty
books were gone. As for nosy Mrs. Zinser, Maud
would tell her about Loraine once the girl decided to
move in with her. The nerve, sitting there all day with
her nose pressed to the window, watching, watching.
It was none of her business if Loraine visited. Of
course, Mrs. Zinser had no idea Maud wasn't in when
Loraine came. Maud could get away up the alley and
to the bus stop without being seen by Mrs. Zinser.

"She's my niece," was all she said.

"I stopped by on Wednesday but you were out," Loraine said.

"I was playing bridge."

"Every Wednesday."

"Like a clock."

As the months passed, Maud regretted that she had been so short with Mrs. Zinser. If Loraine had ever come to the house again when she wasn't home, she left no trace of her visit. Not one. When she came home from bridge, Maud went through the house, asking aloud, "Was Loraine here today? Did Loraine come to see me today?"

When she signed up for the three-day trip to Las Vegas, Maud asked Loraine to stop by the house and water the plants. She dropped the better part of a thousand dollars in Vegas, but it was worth it. Honestly, in those three days she'd had a total of maybe ten hours sleep. She stuck to the slot machines until her arm was sore and she was out a packet, but she was nonetheless happy when she got back. The first thing she did was check the plants. She smiled. They were all moist.

"Your niece is married, I see," Mrs. Zinser said, when they bumped into one another in an aisle of the supermarket.

"Oh, no. She's single."

"Engaged?" Mrs. Zinser was frowning.

Maud ignored her, moving majestically toward a counter where jams and jellies stood. What on earth was Mrs. Zinser talking about? Silly old busybody.

But Mrs. Zinser's question took on new meaning
when the black police detective came to the door and
asked if she could have a few words with Maud.

Maud's first reaction was one of guilt. Her gambling life, while perfectly legal, violated some more
basic code. From time to time, Maud was bothered by
the fact that hers was a silly life, a life of games and
diversion and self-indulgence. She asked the detective
to come in.

FIFTEEN

IT WAS THE KIND OF DETAIL Phil Keegan did not like, and it was particularly annoying to have Agnes going on about it in front of Cy.

"What you're saying is that you've established an alibi for Chris Bourke," he interrupted.

Even Cy seemed to be taking inordinate interest in the fact that Loraine Howells had used her aunt's house as a place of assignation with Chris Bourke. As far as Keegan was concerned, nothing that bastard did would surprise him, but in the case in point, the alibi that Bourke had offered, lunch with Roger Dowling, was more than adequately complemented by his afternoon of dalliance with Loraine Howells.

"The neighbor, Mrs. Zinser, says they've been there before. She thinks they're visiting the aunt, Maud Kaiser. At least she did."

"We already know they were there," Phil said, relighting his cigar. He had let it go out in deference to Agnes's rabbit act with her nose at the beginning of the meeting. "Cy followed them. So what have we gained?"

Agnes was more perturbed by the cigar than by his impatience. "The aunt goes on and on about what a marvelous young lady her niece is. Rose right to the top in television. Whatever you or I might think of

EH," Agnes went on, apparently mimicking the aunt, "it would not have the polish and popularity it has if it weren't for Loraine." She went on in her own voice, "That's Loraine, as in quiche."

"She only knows what the niece tells her."

"Not quite."

"How so?"

"She has met Craig Wilhelms. He came to see her to talk about her niece. Said it was company policy, getting an employee's family perspective. Said it helps them in ensuring that the employee's career progresses in the proper manner."

"Is that company policy?"

"It looks like it was invented by Craig Wilhelms for this occasion. No one else ever heard of it."

Keegan had to agree that this was an interesting wrinkle. "What do you make of it, Agnes?"

"Just guessing?"

"Whatever."

"It could be a jealous man checking up to see what his ladylove's been doing. Or an ambitious employee keeping tabs on his boss."

"Have you checked that out?"

"I wanted to report to you first."

"See if you can find Wilhelms's motive."

"What did you learn from Father Dowling?"

Keegan drew on his cigar. It had been a mistake to tell Agnes he would be working with her when he interviewed Roger Dowling. The woman had a very literal mind.

"Bourke had been to the rectory before the daughter disappeared."

"To see Father Dowling?"

"They were in the seminary together." He said it as if to suggest that there were arcane Catholic implications in the remark that Agnes could not be expected to understand.

"They stayed in touch?"

"Hardly. Did you ever watch Bourke's program?"

"I'll stick with Dr. Ruth."

"Who's Dr. Ruth?"

Agnes looked at Cy. "Is he serious?"

Ten minutes later, Phil dismissed them. His cigar was down to an inch and a half and he would have liked to light another, but what was the point, without Agnes there to annoy? He owed himself two more cigars, and he decided to save them for that evening, when he visited the St. Hilary rectory. The Cubs were playing a night game at Wrigley and he and Roger were going to watch it on television.

"HAVE YOU MET Craig Wilhelms yet?" Roger asked.

"Just this afternoon." It was what he had done instead of having a cigar after the meeting with Agnes and Cy.

"Tell me about it."

Undeniably, Craig was an interesting piece of the puzzle. Tuttle's story, if it was true, made him more fascinating still: The man who had lured Tuttle to the warehouse while the body of Sonya Bourke was put in the back seat.

"What can you tell me about the dead girl?" Phil asked Wilhelms after his secretary had reluctantly shown him into her boss's office. Craig didn't rise from the chair behind the desk, but he did watch Phil cross the room to him.

"I'm not a good source for information about her, Captain."

"Why not?"

"I hardly knew her."

"How long have you worked here?"

"From the beginning, but that doesn't—"

"Beginning of what?"

"Of the program."

"Then you would have seen her off and on over the years. I mean, how often has she been on the program?"

"Do you want an exact figure?"

"Fairly often?"

"Not in the past several years."

"Why not?"

"I guess she grew out of it."

"What do you know about her becoming a Catholic?"

Once in a while during an interview you stumble on something, and this was one of those times. Wilhelms had been sullen before, but now he became fidgety, and color rose to suffuse his face.

"Why would I know anything about that?"

"You tell me."

Wilhelms was squirming now, and though Phil couldn't figure out why, it was an advantage he might just as well exploit.

"Why did you lie about Tuttle?"

"Lie? I didn't lie. I told you I threw him out of here and I did. You can ask Miss Bice."

"We've already asked Miss Bice."

"All right." He made a gesture indicating he considered the matter settled.

"I'm inclined to believe Tuttle."

"But that's absurd."

"I don't suppose you realize that one of my men was down there. He had followed Tuttle."

"I don't believe you."

"You're saying I'm a liar."

"No. Of course not. What I mean is that it doesn't change one thing if you had an army of police on the scene."

"One was enough. This man is particularly keen-eyed."

If anyone had reported to Keegan the use of such tactics, the captain of detectives would have read the riot act to him. Peanuts had seen no one but Tuttle. But at the moment Keegan was only interested in seeing Wilhelms squirm.

"Mr. Wilhelms, I have a favor to ask of you. I want you to go down to the warehouse with me and show me around."

Wilhelms sat back and seemed to be regaining his composure. "I'm not in charge of warehouses, Captain."

"I thought you were the number-two man around here, in charge of everything."

"Only in a sense. I deal with few things directly."

"You know where the warehouse is, don't you?"

"Of course."

"And you've been there?"

"Chris and I looked it over before we signed the lease."

"EH doesn't own the property?"

A bad question, it put Craig Wilhelms completely at ease, as he began to recite the terms of EH's agreement with the owner of the warehouse.

"You got a key to the place?"

"If you have a search warrant."

Wilhelms might have meant it as a joke, but Keegan dropped the warrant on his desk.

"Since you're in charge, I want you to show me around."

"You might have told me at the outset you had a warrant."

"That's true."

At the warehouse, Keegan had the sense he'd been there before, a sense gained from pondering Tuttle's account of being led into the dark by Wilhelms. On this occasion, after unlocking the door, Craig reached in and switched on a light, but in the moment before he did Keegan got a sense of how dark it was without it. They had come into a narrow area, and at right angles to the outside door, perhaps twenty feet away, was another door. It had only a lock, no handle. Tuttle had certainly set the scene with accuracy.

Wilhelms pushed through the second door, holding it for Keegan, and they were in a vast echoing space filled with television props. At the far end were large metal doors that opened when Wilhelms entered some numbers on a little keypad revealed by lifting the lid of a metal box. They stood on the dock and looked across the asphalt expanse toward the weedy field beyond and Keegan tried to imagine Wilhelms sprinting across it after he had abandoned Tuttle inside the warehouse.

"You made one mistake, Wilhelms." He waited until the man turned to him. "You shouldn't have written that note on the back of Tuttle's business card."

To Keegan's surprise, Craig Wilhelms laughed and was suddenly more relaxed than he had been since Keegan was admitted to his office.

"There is no such card, Captain Keegan."

"How could he be sure you didn't have it unless he himself got it back?" Roger Dowling asked, when Phil recounted to him his meeting with Craig Wilhelms.

"Taking it from Tuttle's car?"

"You don't think so?"

"I don't think Wilhelms took it."

"Aha."

Silence fell in the rectory study as, through dense clouds of tobacco smoke, the slow ritual of the televised game continued and two old friends communed beyond the need of words. Roger would know that he did not know who had taken the business card from

the front seat of Tuttle's car. The shadowy figure or
figures were the same one or ones who had placed the
dead body of Sonya in the back seat. Surrounded by
books that to him were unintelligible—theological
tomes, commentaries on canon law, literature of the
kind Keegan had always regarded a task rather than a
pleasure—the Fox River policeman felt momentarily
attracted by the long view those books provided. There
was a final sorting out of sheep from goats; eventually sin was punished and merit rewarded. There was
one whose watchful eye no deed escaped. So viewed,
it seemed a smaller matter that other creatures did not
know which creature or creatures had made such a
mockery of the corpse of the young woman. No one
who knew Tuttle could imagine that he would be seriously suspected as Sonya's murderer. Not that Keegan took this on faith. Agnes had put together an
account of Tuttle's comings and goings during a two-
day period that most certainly included the fateful
moment when someone had driven a narrow pointed
instrument into Sonya's heart. When Keegan's eye
went down the schedule he had the sense of looking
over the shoulder of the Recording Angel. My God,
how little Tuttle's life toted up to when reduced to this
bare account. Between Chinese restaurants and junk-
food franchises, Tuttle spent an enormous amount of
time eating. And with Pianone. Keegan had known
the two men were acquaintances, but Agnes's account revealed that they were companions, friends.
They were often together in restaurants, if these two
days were typical. What did not strike the eye was

much legal business. Oh, Tuttle was in his office every day, but there was no record of clients coming and going.

"Did you check his phone calls?" he asked Agnes.

"All outgoing calls."

"Let me see them."

The supplementary list revealed that Tuttle had food brought in as well, one pizza order and a call to the Orient Express. Keegan consulted the other list. That must be the order Tuttle called for. Where the hell were the man's clients?

One of the calls was to Amos Cadbury's office. Keegan looked up at Agnes.

"I checked there. He asked to speak to Mr. Cadbury."

"And?"

"The call was never returned."

That could be Tuttle's epitaph. How did the man afford even the simple diet he was on?

Sitting in the rectory study, Keegan knew that they had made no progress in the discovery of the killer of Sonya Bourke. One of the truly depressing things about his work was the number of crimes destined to remain forever a mystery. Perhaps that's why the long view attracted.

SIXTEEN

EDDIE HILL had been the despair of his elders when he was a kid, never doing in school what he should be doing, given his test scores. Counselor after counselor had spoken in hushed tones of those test scores. The trouble was they would never reveal them to Eddie, who didn't see why they didn't just give him credit for the scores and leave him alone.

"You're college potential, Eddie."

When Eddie was a sophomore in high school, Miss Scriptor, the meatless wonder, had tried to instil ambition in him and get him excited about a future that included more school.

"School bores me."

"Of course it does. You're not being challenged. Once we would have been able to skip you ahead, but not now." Miss Scriptor scowled at the days in which they were doomed to live. "You must challenge yourself."

She let up a bit when he told her he read a lot. Eddie spent a lot of time in the library just to get away from the chaos of his home. His father drank and his mother worked, and he didn't want to know what his older brothers and sisters were up to. Whenever two or more Hills gathered together, there was a fight, a noisy fight. The library was preferable to that.

"De Quincey?" Miss Scriptor asked.

"He's an English writer."

"Confessions of an English Opium Eater," she breathed.

"I haven't gotten to that yet."

Miss Scriptor seemed surprised to learn De Quincey had written lots of things. De Quincey's essays on Coleridge and Wordsworth and Johnson had sent Eddie to those writers. He liked them but he always went back to the Americans, Cooper and Twain, Irving and Hawthorne. Miss Scriptor made a snoring sound as she breathed with open mouth. Eddie couldn't make her understand that his reading had nothing to do with school. He hated school.

In his junior year he volunteered for the Marine Corps, went through boot in San Diego, spent his year in Nam, acquiring a headful of images he spent a lot of time suppressing, came out of the Corps with a bundle, got a chauffeur's license and began driving for Lux-o-Limo, kept on saving, and was about to buy his own vehicle when the job with EH came along. The rest was history.

Bourke hired a stretch from Lux-o-Limo fairly often and began to request Eddie as his driver.

"I'm going to own my own limo," Eddie told him.

"Don't you want my business?"

"Then I could drive for you full time."

Bourke smiled in the back. "How much does one of these things cost?"

"You'd be surprised."

"Surprise me."

Bourke didn't even blink at the number. Eddie hadn't thought he would. He'd checked out EH, he'd watched a few programs and concluded that Bourke was a snake-oil salesman. Of course it hadn't escaped Eddie's notice that the self-styled sexual liberationist hired the car because of its roomy interior. When Eddie closed off the front seat from the passenger, leaving Bourke enclosed in a leathery mobile bordello, he had little doubt what was going on back there. He had assured Bourke of the utter privacy of the limo. What he meant was that his lips were sealed, not that he couldn't hear. A man of fewer scruples would have taken advantage of being privy to Bourke's indiscretions. Eddie installed a recording system, audio, video, but not for profit. It was only another proof of the overwhelming depravity of human nature.

In the library of the USO in San Francisco he had read Calvin's *Institutes* and for the first time in his life truly felt in tune with the author he read. The Geneva divine had no illusions about mankind; he explained the fact that a human person, if given the chance to do well or badly, is more likely to go wrong, by invoking Original Sin. As far as Eddie was concerned, this was just another name for what Calvin began with. Whether or not you saw that as an explanation, Calvin's diagnosis and description of the race were right on the money so far as Eddie could see. There are those who hold that, of all our weaknesses, the proclivity to misbehave in sexual matters is the least, and they had Dante on their side, but never forget, Eddie lectured an imaginary interlocutor, the great Florentine had consigned Paolo and Francesca to hell. Eddie was not so much scandalized as reassured by Bourke's antics in the back of the limo. Of course, in the case of the television propagandist of libidinous liberty—Eddie harbored a secret admiration for Spiro, or, more accurately, for Buchanan, his muse—it would have been a lapse not to fall, and Eddie had half-hoped that the former priest's hypocrisy would be, having preached fun and games to others, to practice an ascetic abstinence from the flesh himself. Not a bit of it. Bourke might be in his sixth decade, but he was still a determined sexual athlete.

When Eddie escaped his squalid home and unchallenging high school and entered the Corps, he had been saying good-bye as well to the family—the one that had spawned him, and any possible one that would have included himself as paterfamilias. On this most central concern of male and female, Eddie Hill had decided to pass. He would rather put some popcorn in the microwave and curl up with a good book anytime. Not that he had a broad empirical base for the comparison. Once, on leave, he and several buddies had rented a car and spent a week touring the western states and in a little town in Nevada, having lunch in a café, they learned that the town brothel was next door.

"Outside and to your right and up them stairs," said the leathery-faced proprietor. He might have been giving directions to the men's room.

Eddie's companions reacted in the expected manner, all but thumping their chests in anticipation. A silent Eddie accompanied them up the stairs. Indelibly imprinted in his memory was the room in which the madam and her two girls awaited whom it might concern. They perked up at the sound of feet on the stairway and seemed especially delighted to see three men hardly more than boys. A doughlike arm emerging from a short-sleeved blouse lay on the arm of the mohair sofa; a scarcely buttoned blouse revealed the mottled expanse of the madam's bosom. Never had a woman seemed so fleshy to Eddie before. By contrast the girls were scrawny and squirmy, excited as monkeys. Warmish beer was produced, Eddie's companions went down the hall with the monkeys, and Eddie was left with the madam.

"What'll it be, cowboy? You want to wait, or do it with Mama?"

For an answer Eddie stood. The madam's little smile bowed her lips. She extended her hand, needing help to rise. She worked in a room in the front, and it was there, engulfed in flesh that seemed an advertisement for mortality, with the sound of an irate car horn punctuating the effort, that Eddie was initiated into the carnal mysteries.

For ten miles afterward, he grinned and nodded as the others talked about how great it had been. But for Eddie it was good to know that's all it was. The first time he became aware of the apostolate of Christopher Bourke and Janet Gray, he thought of them as bringing to Chicago and beyond the healthy acceptance of the flesh in that little Nevada town.

Driving for Bourke he had seen a parade of temporary alternatives to the consolations offered by Janet Gray, but Loraine Howells was different, though it was difficult to see why. For purposes of a quickie in the back of the limo, there was, Eddie opined, little to choose between this girl and that. Variety and turnover seemed the thing—if you went for that sort of thing. Eddie himself had become a eunuch for the kingdom of peace of mind's sake. He did not want some indiscretion, any bending to momentary passion, to land him in the kind of situation he had joined the Corps to escape. Prevention? The million and a half abortions performed every year suggested that prevention was not the cure-all it was touted to be.

The first thing about Loraine Howells that set her off from the others was that she worked for Bourke, and not just as one of the supernumeraries who came and went, but as the executive producer of the main program. She had accompanied Bourke and others, Craig Wilhelms, for example, on strictly business jaunts in the limo, and her sterile efficiency seemed an extra coat of armor neutralizing her undeniable gender. When the relation between her and Bourke changed, Bourke actually forewarned Eddie that he would want to be shut in even though his companion was Loraine. Eddie's expression did not change. He nodded and, when they were on their way and the request was made, he hit the button and the solid divider rose from the back seat and turned the limo into two separate sections. Of course Eddie listened in. The second way Loraine differed from the others was that

she was in charge, even now the director as much as
the participant.

Eddie did not think this new departure in Bourke's
dalliance boded well. Loraine was not a bimbo. She
was at least as ambitious as Chris and Janet. Further-
more, while Janet had grown old in the battle to stay
young, Loraine was young, thirty at most, not much
younger than Eddie. Odd how she reminded him of
those two monkeys in the upstairs brothel in Nevada.
Sometimes, speculatively, he had asked himself if his
attitude would have been the same if he had waited for
one of the girls rather than chosen the unappetizing
madam.

A driver becomes invisible to those he drives, even
when the divider between front and back is down.
Bourke was always jovial, there was usually a mean-
ingless exchange, but Eddie knew his employer regarded him as little more than an accessory to the
limo. It was the same with Loraine and Craig, when
they used the limo, alone or together. They relied on
his discretion as implicitly as Bourke did, largely because they lost awareness of him in the front seat after they got under way. Anyone in such circumstances
is going to learn a lot to be discreet about. And Eddie, who had a sense of foreboding when the relationship between Bourke and Loraine turned from
business to monkey business, had his fears realized
when it became clear that Loraine and Craig were discussing the impact on themselves of what they took to
be the imminent entry of Sonya into the corporate
scene. Hugh Hefner's daughter, apparently straight as

an arrow, had taken over her father's sex empire and so, they conjectured, might Sonya. Perhaps Sonya seemed more of a threat because she was utterly immune to the EH message. Eddie had always felt an affinity with Sonya and let her ride up front with him because she hated to ride in back. Besides, he had no reason to tape her.

"I feel like a funeral back there."

"I know what you mean."

"Don't you get bored, just driving people? It must be even more boring sitting around waiting."

Eddie showed her the book he was reading. Manzoni's *I Promessi Sposi*.

"What language is that?"

"Italian."

"You're not Italian, are you?"

Eddie smiled. He had a reading knowledge of six languages but it would have been showy to say so. "I picked it up."

She was leafing through the book, a bemused smile on her lips. From then on, driving Sonya was anything but boring.

"Did you know you've got an intellectual for a driver," she said once, when she was in back with her father. But Eddie looked at her in the rearview mirror and she got away from it. Bourke thought it was some kind of joke and didn't pursue it.

"That was dumb, Eddie," she told him later. "I'm sorry. I'll keep your secret."

"You plan to come into the business when you finish college?"

The way she looked at him she didn't have to say anything. Eddie felt a surprising relief. Why should he care what Sonya Bourke did with her life? But if Sonya kept his secret, he kept hers. Astounding as it appeared at first, there was little doubt that the daughter of Chris Bourke and Janet Gray had got religion.

The human comedy, it had been called, and sitting in the limo, before he picked up his current book, Eddie would muse on the tangled and unpredictable situation at EH. The boss was getting in deeper and deeper with Loraine, unaware that she and Craig were concerned about the plans he might have for Sonya. If Bourke thought his daughter would join the family enterprise, he was in for a disappointment, but nothing like the one he would know if he discovered that she had begun to frequent Catholic churches. That gave her a guilty secret in common with Craig Wilhelms, but of course neither of them could know it. Calvin, thou shouldst be living at this hour. It seemed a sign of perversity of mankind that two people connected with an enterprise meant to exalt the flesh should have turned to a religion even Calvinists regarded as repressive in that department. Can one be tempted by the good?

"Eddie," Janet Gray said from the back one day, "who besides Mr. Bourke and myself have a claim on this car?"

"Whoever else you say."

Her smile looked like an advertisement for lipstick, perfect teeth framed by glistening scarlet. "Of course

Craig can call on you if you're not otherwise engaged."

"Mr. Wilhelms definitely."

"Loraine Howells?"

"Only with someone else."

"Mr. Bourke?"

Eddie had seen it coming. Janet was a shrewd woman and tolerant of her husband's philandering—how in the name of EH could she object?—but tolerance had hitherto involved only fugitive flings. It was inevitable that she should have known of Loraine and known it was not the same as the others. Calvin had been right about predestination too. We think we're free because the plot of the play we're in is hidden from us. Eddie did not like to think where all this was leading.

"Or Mr. Wilhelms."

"Do you keep a log of your trips, Eddie?"

"Only here." He tapped his head.

"Eddie, I have a very unusual request to make of you."

He listened, keeping his expression impassive. Janet Gray wanted him to report to her on trips Bourke took with Loraine.

"I gather you drop them off sometimes."

Eddie said nothing.

"You have a phone in the car. Give me a ring the next time."

Their eyes locked in the mirror. Eddie felt mesmerized. He felt he was predestined to nod in agreement. The whole thing had been settled from all eternity.

SEVENTEEN

MAUD WOULD HAVE PREFERRED expelling from her mind the knowledge that Loraine had abused her hospitality, bringing a man to the house in her absence, and a disgraceful man like Christopher Bourke at that. Maud did not practice the religion she had taken on with her marriage and dropped when she became a widow, but she retained enough Catholic sensibility to object strongly to what Bourke and his wife said about the Church on their program. Of course she watched it, fascinated, horrified, hooked. Honestly, the things they talked about, as if it were the most natural thing in the world. "Pleasuring." The word did not seem to cover her joyless encounters with Merle, and Maud wondered if something essential was missing from her life. Well, it was too late now, and she didn't care what the little old ladies on the show said about their sex lives.

Sex lives! Did people talk about their digestive lives? Their cardiovascular lives? Maud was shocked. It was difficult to believe her niece was connected with such a production, but Maud convinced herself that Loraine had a neutral skill that could be employed by any television program, regardless of content. She was helped in this by Loraine's dismissal of all inquiries about EH.

"Watch the program if you want to know."

"I have better things to do with my time."

"So do I."

"Why do you work there?"

"Because they pay me well."

It was just a job, that's what Maud took this answer to mean. Why, she herself probably knew more about the program than Loraine did.

And now to learn that Loraine was having an affair with the high priest of sex himself and using her house for the purpose! She felt crushed, used. She stared at the black policewoman, and it seemed doubly demeaning to have to discuss such a matter with her.

"You weren't home at the time?" Officer Lamb asked.

"Certainly not."

"Well, one of the neighbors confirms they were here. The rendezvous turns out to be his alibi."

"Alibi!"

"His daughter was murdered about that time."

She let Maud figure it out. But why on earth would they think even Christopher Bourke would murder his own daughter?

"It doesn't matter now. He was here with his girlfriend when the daughter was killed."

Maud would not give her the satisfaction of being angry at this remark, and she had the feeling that the officer was trying to disturb her, as if she might, when out of temper, tell her things about Loraine and Bourke.

The phone began to ring before Officer Lamb drove off but Maud refused to answer. She was sure it was the busybody next door and she wouldn't give her the satisfaction either. In the back of her mind she began to think of places to go; she had to get out of town. Vegas? Perhaps. But what about Acapulco or Guadalajara? Somewhere exotic would be nice. The phone continued to ring but Maud ignored it, thinking of palm trees, dry heat, a row of one-armed bandits.

When the front bell sounded, Maud peeked out the dining-room window and saw Barney standing at the door. Dear God! Her slovenly son slouched as he stood, his lips working in and out of a sneering smile. Or was he rehearsing what he would say to her? But Barney was flesh and blood, support of a kind in this time of embarrassment. She had never thought of her son in this way before and it had been sufficiently long since she saw him that the delusion lasted while she unbolted the front door and opened it to him.

"Is this the Kaiser Hot-Sheet Hotel?" he cried as he came in, his head cocked, as if he were addressing the world.

"Barney!" But even his insolence was welcome now. Better to be insulted by her son than by a police officer.

He went right on to the kitchen as if he could once more claim seigneurial rights here, as if she hadn't locked him out of the house and told him she wanted to see him no more. She tried to find in that huge shuffling figure the infant she had borne, had fed at her breast, fussed over and dreamed dreams of. Dear

God. Look at him now. Maud felt that she had given birth to a hippopotamus. He opened the refrigerator and stooped to inspect its contents.

"Why don't you have something to eat?" Maud said sarcastically.

"You feed the customers between bouts?"

"Barney, stop that. I should think you at least would have some kind of..."

He straightened and turned slowly, his brows raised in expectation. He waited. "Some kind of compassion?"

"Feeling, yes."

"As in throwing your only son into the street while Loraine is given the run of the house, or at least the bedrooms, entertaining your favorite television star?"

"You always defended Bourke."

"I never pimped for him."

Maud burst into tears, welcome tears, the ultimate defense. Barney was a dreadful boy. Boy! He was a young man. By the looks of him he continued to live a useless life, unkempt hair hanging greasily over his pale forehead, stubble bristling the fat folds of his face, little pouched eyes gleaming malevolently at her from thirty years of self-pity. Was it her fault he was so fat? There was no obesity on her side of the family. Nor on Merle's either. Where had Barney's size come from? When he was a boy, she would say that he had glandular trouble, not knowing what that was supposed to mean. She had nightmares of a Grimm Brothers kind in which wicked witches took her true child and put Barney in the crib in his place. Barney was the product of some unnatural coupling of beast and man, not the fruit of her womb. She awoke from such dreams feeling a frightening mixture of fear and relief. How she had hated the year Barney studied nothing but psychology and busied himself with analyzing her.

"You imagine I'm not really your child, don't you?" he asked one day.

"You're no longer a child."

"It's the reverse of the child's dream that he was kidnapped and is living with adoptive parents."

"Is that your dream?"

This phase passed, all Barney's phases passed. She asked what he was studying now.

"Pornography."

"Be serious."

"Oh, I am. I feel like a Martian come to this strange planet, trying to understand the behavior of the inhabitants. Their method of reproduction seems sensible enough, but what I cannot understand is their obsession with one another's genitals. Take Loraine and Christopher Bourke." He raised his empty hand to stop her; the other hand held a milk carton from which he had been drinking. "Here is a man who has made a fortune telling others that their purpose in life is the pursuit of pleasure. By which he means, ignore the mind, ignore the imagination, ignore even the human ingenuity that produced the technology that enables him to beam this message across the nation;

forget all that, and scratch yourselves or one another. Do it with the dog, whatever works.''

Despite herself, Maud laughed. She sat at the kitchen table, drying her eyes.

"Has it been on the news?''

"The house of ill fame on Curzon Street? It's in the papers.''

"My God.''

"Oh, they went lightly on you. They had a more difficult task trying to make a man who said he would take it wherever he found it seem newsworthy because he was diddling his producer when his daughter was killed.''

"The house was mentioned?''

"The address. I had almost forgotten it, and then I remembered.'' He brought a fat hand slapping against his head. "The ancestral manse. Of course I rushed right home to be of what help I could.'' The edges of his smile collided with his cheeks and formed a dark little rectangle. "It is so good to be under the family roof again.''

Hateful a son as he was, Maud felt no repugnance at the thought of his coming home again. She had tried to forget him and adopt Loraine as her child and heir, and look at the thanks she had been given. Barney was an embarrassment, but had he publicly embarrassed her the way Loraine had? No. The neighbors whispered about him, the great fat son who seemed caught in an interlude, a student beyond the proper years for it, going nowhere and in no hurry to get there. His bitterness and cruel remarks were better than loneliness, loneliness or gambling.

"I'm going to the track in an hour."

He licked Miracle Whip from his fingers. "I'd like that. Who's running today?"

EIGHTEEN

EVER SINCE HE HAD BEEN led up the garden path by Craig Wilhelms and found the body of the Bourke girl in his car, Tuttle had been engaged in all but continual consultation with his dead father, the other Tuttle in Tuttle & Tuttle. Tuttle *fils* accused himself of stupidity, and worse, while Tuttle *père* assured him that he had acted according to the highest standards of the profession, and that what had happened to him could have happened to any lawyer.

Tuttle tried to imagine it happening to Amos Cadbury, the Platonic ideal of the lawyer for Fox River, Illinois. He phoned Cadbury, wanting to make an appointment, but had predictable difficulty with his receptionist, the juiceless Miss Cleary.

"I'd like to leave a message."

"Very well."

"I need legal representation. Mr. Cadbury will have read of my plight."

"Is Tuttle spelled with two *t*'s?

"Three," he croaked.

Her tone of voice consigned Tuttle to some outer darkness where reptilian creatures slithered in the slime. Even on his best days, Tuttle had no defense against that tone, and in his present funk it made mincemeat of his self-respect. He hung up and looked at the phone, suddenly appreciative of clients who had just made their one phone call and awaited an advocate to restore freedom to them.

In his despondency, Tuttle had been avoiding Peanuts. This made no sense. Thank God for Peanuts. Where would he be without the little cop's corroboration of his story? But Peanuts reminded him of his humiliation downtown, an officer of the court suddenly put in the position of one of society's outcast. A dead body found in his Toyota!

It could happen to anyone, said Tuttle *père,* and Tuttle *fils* did not believe it for a minute.

"Out on parole, Tuttle?"

It was that taunting remark of Tetzel in the press room that broke the spell, galvanizing Tuttle and returning him to his normal ebullient self. The best defense is a good offense. He invited Peanuts to his office for a pizza.

"What's being done about Craig Wilhelms?"

"Who's he?"

"The son of a bitch who lured me to that warehouse."

Bourke had once kept someone named Virginia Verona locked up, and Wilhelms would show Tuttle where she had been kept. The idea seemed to be that this was where Bourke's daughter might be found. If Wilhelms had wanted to give Tuttle a taste of what such confinement is like, he had succeeded.

Peanuts chomped on a wedge of pizza and pulled it from his mouth, creating a cat's cradle of mozzarella. He studied Tuttle as he chewed.

"He lured me to that warehouse and when we went to my car, there was the body of the girl. Think, Peanuts. Did you see anyone else around that warehouse? Did you see another car?"

It was not reassuring to see Peanuts stop chewing and screw his face into an effort to think.

"What kind of car was it?"

Good question. No one else had asked him that. He closed his eyes and relived that moment when the bumper touched the back of his leg and he turned to see Craig Wilhelms emerging from the car. From the passenger side! Was he imagining that? No, he was sure of it. So there had to have been someone else with him, at least one other person, the driver of the car. But something in his memory rejected the possibility of more than one other person. Why? A sports car. He had the definite impression of a sports car!

From his chair on the other side of the desk, Peanuts was watching him intently. Tuttle realized he was holding a cooling piece of pizza. He sat forward.

"Peanuts, I want you to do something. I want you to check out the vehicles registered to..." To whom? "To everybody connected with EH."

"The movie?"

Tuttle stared dumbfounded at his friend. What in the hell movie could Peanuts be thinking of? Patience, patience. He crammed the pizza into his mouth, took a swig of Pepsi and began to make a list. Bourke, Janet Gray, Craig Wilhelms, the son of a bitch, and who else? The producer, Loraine What-

chamacallit. Loraine Howells. And Craig's secretary.
For the first time in days, Tuttle felt on top of things.

"Have some more pizza, Peanuts," he said, shov-
ing the carton across the desk. Peanuts shifted the
piece he held to his left hand and reached for another.
"I'll come over there with you and we'll check this
through together. After all, I am still technically under suspicion."

But that burden was lifted forever. Tuttle was back
in business, on the offensive, and his mind began to
move along familiar grooves. He knew Craig Wilhelms had been to the warehouse and now he knew
someone else had driven him there, but this knowledge was useless without proof. With proof, well,
Tuttle smiled slyly, with proof, who knew what he
might do with such knowledge?

THERE WAS A FIERO registered in the name of Miss
Bice, Craig's secretary. Tuttle jotted down her address, and that night, with Peanuts at the wheel of a
patrol car, turned in at the driveway of a pleasant little home in Skokie.

"You wait here," he said to Peanuts, deciding
against asking him to turn on the gum ball. He made
as much noise as he could slamming the door of the
squad car and sauntered toward the front door with
his tweed hat pulled low over his eyes.

"What is it?" The man in the doorway wore a
sweatshirt and an old pair of pants flecked with paint
and his feet were bare. He was about fifty.

"Your daughter Hazel home?"

"Who are you?" But he looked past Tuttle to the patrol car parked prominently at the curb.

"Fox River Police. I'd like to question your daughter."

"Question her?"

What a sense of power police must have. Tuttle knew the man would have liked to slam the door in his face, but he couldn't do that, not to the police. He stepped to one side, and Tuttle went in.

"This shouldn't take long." He stood in the middle of the room looking around, then headed for the television and turned it off. The man did not object. Tuttle knew he was in charge.

Hazel Bice came downstairs with a towel wrapped around her just-washed hair. "You're not police," she said, shocked.

"I want to talk to you before they get in on it. They're outside."

"I have nothing to say."

"Hazel, I know you drove Craig Wilhelms to the warehouse the day he arranged to meet me there. You damned near ran me down when you pulled up."

She slumped onto the couch. "I never said I didn't."

"That's true. And that's in your favor. I promise you that. What do you know about the body of Sonya Bourke?"

"Nothing! I swear."

"He didn't explain to you that was the point of the exercise?"

"It wasn't."

"Oh, come on."

"Mr. Wilhelms can explain it to you."

"We like to have several accounts of the same facts."

She shook her head and the towel came loose. As she was wrapping it around her hair again she began to cry.

"That's enough," her father said.

"Not quite. I want you to put what you said in writing."

"She doesn't have to do that."

"Tell your father I'm a lawyer, Hazel."

"You told me you were the police."

"With the police. I said I was with the police. You saw the squad car. Would you rather have your daughter taken downtown?"

"What do you want her to write?"

"That she drove Craig Wilhelms to the warehouse and saw him take me inside."

Her father looked at her. "Stop crying. Write that down, for God's sake. Let's get this over with. I want that damned police car out of here."

Of course he would be worried about the neighbors. Tuttle sympathized with him. He sympathized a lot more when Hazel scribbled some lines on a piece of paper torn from a steno pad. "I drove Mr. Wilhelms to the EH warehouse on Wednesday, April 10, to meet Mr. Tuttle and saw them go inside together. Then I left."

"Where did you go when you left?"

"I came right home. He told me to and I did."

"Good girl."

His praise puzzled her, for that matter Tuttle himself was surprised when the words emerged from his mouth. But it was her written statement that made him grateful.

Her father went before him to the door, opened it and looked out. Did he expect to see his neighbors congregating in the street, gawking at his daughter? Apparently the coast was clear. He waved Tuttle through.

"Mission accomplished," he said as he slid in beside Peanuts.

"Listen to this."

Peanuts fiddled with the radio, not the police radio, the regular radio. Still holding the exonerating paper, Tuttle cocked an ear to humor Peanuts. What he heard made him very glad he had gotten the statement from Hazel Bice when he had.

Craig Wilhelms had committed suicide.

NINETEEN

THE PATRICIAN FIGURE of Amos Cadbury appeared
at the door of the St. Hilary rectory the following
Sunday just when Roger Dowling had risen from the
table after his noonday meal, a repast Marie called
brunch, as if to disclaim all responsibility for serving
scrambled eggs and bacon at this hour of the day.

"If you'd come earlier, you could have joined me
for brunch."

"Thank you, Father. Can you spare a minute?"

Roger gestured toward the parlor but something in
Amos's reaction made him suggest they talk in the
study. Amos visibly brightened.

"Of course, 'parlor' means talking room," Roger
Dowling said as they went down the hall.

"Does it, Father. I hadn't known that."

"It's not a fact of much importance."

"I have come to think that all facts have their importance. It is true that there are times when we don't
see or grasp their importance, but that is another
matter."

Amos Cadbury was precise in the most casual moments of life, as if the skills of a lawyer must never be
allowed to get rusty.

"I wish to speak to you as one lawyer to another,
Father."

"You flatter me."

"On the contrary. The little I know of canon law leads me to hold its practitioners in high regard."

Roger Dowling decided against reminding Amos that his days as a canon lawyer were happily in the past. Amos was setting a scene and it was advisable to let him proceed as he wished. He looked wistfully at the box of cigars Roger Dowling offered him.

"How lovely they look."

"They're Miami Cubans."

"If you wouldn't consider it a waste, I would like one. Not to smoke—alas, I have managed to put that behind me. Just to hold."

"Of course."

Amos unwrapped the cigar and passed in under his narrow nose, eyes closed, inhaling ecstatically.

"I'll light my pipe."

Amos watched him as he did, avidly, hungrily. Well, to be in the rectory study while the pastor smoked was in effect to smoke. Roger hoped he was not leading Amos astray.

"I believe we both know a lawyer named Tuttle, Father."

Roger Dowling nodded, still puffing his pipe to life.

"I have to accuse myself of profound uncharitableness in his regard. He has tried to see me and I have avoided him. I know it must have something to do with this tragic business with the priest's daughter and I simply do not want to get mixed up in it. I hope you can understand my reasons. These past several decades have been painful for a Catholic raised as I was,

Father. I grew up in a world where nuns and priests were so far above suspicion, it would have seemed accusatory even to say they were above suspicion. It went without saying. I lived to see priests abandon the clerical life and nuns flee from the convents, all of this explained in ways I found, and find, unintelligible. But if that has been a cross, the case of Christopher Bourke and Janet Gray is far, far worse. If I could imagine it, I would not even think of it. But their sin should not be heaped on their daughter's shoulders. I should be Christian enough to do what I can, even if that means dealing with the despicable Tuttle.''

"What do you want from me, Amos?"

"Advice."

"I am not going to tell you that you have an obligation to work with Tuttle."

"Oh, that is no longer the question. I have been contacted by Janet Gray. I speak, of course, in confidence."

"Of course," Roger Dowling said, for Marie's benefit if she was tuned in from the kitchen, which was highly probable.

"Father, as you may know, I have never accepted divorce cases. This is only partly a matter of principle. I would be less than frank if I did not say that such cases are invariably acrimonious and the client you help resents it and half blames you for his troubles. But even if those things were not true, I would not take a divorce case."

Roger Dowling waited.

"This is my problem. Janet Gray wishes to divorce Christopher Bourke. It would be what is nowadays called a media event. Those two have turned themselves inside out in public, made what decent folk recognize as private the very stuff of their television program. And they have made a very good thing out of slandering the Church. The lawyer who has either of those two as a client is a fool."

"So you refused."

Amos again held the cigar under his nose for a moment. "My partners are furious that I have not already done so. The firm does not need business, we need not pursue publicity cynically in order to attract other clients, it would be positively harmful. There are clients of long standing whose loyalty might waver if I should represent Janet Gray in this action."

"But you are tempted?"

"Father Dowling, you may be one of the few men left who can understand my hesitation. I have not attempted to explain it to others. Of course I need not. I am to my partners as Lincoln was to his cabinet. As for losing clients, I lose some every day to the grave and there are always others to take their place. Who but yourself will grasp that I do not see this as a divorce case?"

Amos picked up a box of matches, took one and struck it. His eyes were hooded as he brought the match to the end of the cigar. Just before tobacco would have begun to burn, he took away the match and blew it out.

"I hope that was not moral gymnastics, Amos. Temptations are frequent enough without fabricating them."

"I never thought I would hear you speak of smoking as a vice, Father. No, it was a moment of weakness." He laid the unlit cigar on the table beside his chair. "It is true that they are in a civil marriage, but even to have contracted that added to their crime. The status of each of them in canon law made marriage impossible and to flaunt the judgment of the Church and have recourse to a civil marriage worsened matters. Nonetheless, the civil marriage had legal standing. To be free of one another legally, they must obtain a divorce. But they are not really married."

"I follow you, Amos."

"Few would, Father. And most would regard the explanation as humbug."

"I suppose."

Amos stirred in his chair and let his eye travel along a shelf of books before looking through the clouds of tobacco smoke at Father Dowling. "But not all. If such thoughts had come to me unbidden, as I believe they would, that would be one thing. But they were prompted by Janet Gray herself."

"How so?"

"She came to me as, in her words, the premier Catholic lawyer in the Chicago area. Pure bunk, of course, but it was not just idle flattery. It is because of my faith that she wants me to represent her. As a Catholic I can be instrumental in rectifying a standing insult to the religious life."

"Does she plan to return to the convent?" Roger Dowling smiled sardonically.

Amos rose angularly, leaned forward and pushed the study door closed. "That is precisely what she says she plans to do, Father Dowling."

Roger's first reaction to this revelation was to think that twenty years of perfidy had made Janet and Chris capable of pretending anything. A cynical appeal to another's faith to achieve her ends would scarcely be beyond a woman who for years on television had been slandering the good women who give their lives to God in the religious life. That the religious life itself had deteriorated during that period was another matter, but in the era to which Janet referred, the religious life had been lived faithfully and well, in many cases even in holiness. Of course she would know the effect of her libel on a man like Amos Cadbury and would know that an appeal to him to rectify it would be all but irresistible. And here sat Amos Cadbury in an agony of conscience, not wanting to violate the principles of a professional lifetime but at the same time not wanting to miss an opportunity to redress the balance so far as the EH onslaught on the Church was concerned. But to suggest that she herself . . .

"Do you believe her, Amos?"

"I do. Incredible and fantastic as it seems, despite the most profound distaste for the idea of representing her, I cannot think she is insincere when she tells me her deepest desire is to devote the rest of her life to making up for the evil she has done."

Amos Cadbury was no fool. If wishes were horses, he would have ridden rapidly away in the opposite direction. Roger had no doubt of that. There lurked in the Cadbury breast no quasi-senile passion to make a splash by denying the convictions of a lifetime.

"Tell me more, Amos. What exactly did she say?"

Amos looked intently at Roger Dowling. "I would rather have her tell you herself. Will you see her?"

"Have you suggested this to her?"

"I hope you will find what I say incompatible with my beliefs on the requirements of gallantry. Even as we speak, she is sitting outside in my car. Heavily veiled, I might add. She did not wish to be recognized when she attended your Mass."

If Roger had ever had any doubts about Amos's reputation for seemingly undramatic yet devastating peripeties in his courtroom presentations, he would have discarded them then. Some version of the problem Amos had described as his own, a reprise of the difficulty he had faced with Chris Bourke, confronted Roger Dowling now. But of course he could not say no.

He stood. "Let's invite the lady inside."

As they left the study, Amos said, "In the parlor perhaps, Father? She retains her puritanical attitude toward tobacco."

But the dramatic encounter was destined not to take place. A minute later an abjectly apologetic Amos returned to say his client was not yet ready to discuss her situation with a priest. Roger Dowling tried not to show his relief.

"Who is that woman?" Marie asked when Father Dowling went on back to the kitchen. If he had meant to tease her about the visitor they'd almost had, her question chased the thought away.

"I can't see her."

"Would you come and have a look? She's been hanging around the side door of the church for twenty minutes."

He went to the back door to look. A woman no longer young, not a member of the parish—Marie would have recognized her if she were.

"Should I go find out, Father?"

"I will."

"You haven't finished your lunch."

"I've had more than enough." Her eye rose birdlike to his. "Not that it wasn't delicious."

"I'll bet you couldn't tell me now what it was."

"Casserole?"

"That was yesterday!"

He let the screen door bang when he went out onto the porch and then strolled along the walk in the direction of the church, hoping the woman would see him and come to him, but this did not happen. She still stood by the church door when he got there.

"Lovely afternoon."

"Are you the priest?"

He was wearing his cassock and collar. "Roger Dowling. Yes, I'm pastor here."

"I'd like to talk." These might have been words she'd been rehearsing, but she brought them out only with difficulty. "I was a Catholic once."

"There's a bench just over here."

Her tale was a familiar one. She had not so much left the Church as the Church had left her. Her husband had been Catholic and she had become one when they married. After his death, she had drifted away from practice, nothing dramatic, she'd just tapered off because it no longer seemed to matter whether or not she went to Mass. So few people seemed to go anymore.

"It's all very much the same, you know. Essentially."

"In English? I heard you in church. When I went we didn't understand a word of the Mass. It meant so much more."

Roger Dowling smiled despite himself.

"What is your name?"

"Maud Kaiser. I suppose it's my son who bothers me most. He's not even baptized."

"How old is he?"

She figured it out on her fingers. "Thirty-nine."

"What does he do?"

Her laugh was like a bark. "He still calls himself a student."

"Is he enrolled somewhere?"

"He's enrolled everywhere. It's difficult to name a university he hasn't attended. He's finally gotten a job of sorts."

"He sounds like an interesting fellow."

She thought about that. The idea seemed new to her. "I wonder if you're right. He's just a big lazy boy to me. And a rebuke."

"Because you didn't raise him in the Church?"

She nodded. "Sometimes I imagine if he would have turned out completely differently if I'd done my duty."

"Do you think he'd like to talk with me?"

"Would you do that, Father?"

"I'd be delighted."

She heaved a theatrical sigh. "I can't tell you what a relief it is to hear you say that."

"Now what about yourself?"

She looked alarmed. "Oh, I'm all right."

"How long since your last confession?"

"Dear God, I've no idea. I couldn't bear to go into a confessional, Father."

"Right here is good enough."

"Do you mean it?"

"Just tell me about your life since you stopped practicing the faith."

Listening to her, he could not help but think how innocent she was. One of the flock always, even though the flock might change, she was moved in whatever direction she went by those around her. "The thing is, I don't want to be at odds with God." She dropped her voice further when she mentioned her gambling.

"Gambling isn't a sin, Maud."

"Maybe not, but it's stupid."

He gave her absolution and then they sat on there. She was a very different woman from the nervous wretch he had first seen from the kitchen window.

"I know I'll continue to gamble."

"Life's a gamble."

She smiled happily. "It is, isn't it, when you stop to think of it?"

"Tell me about Barney."

"Oh, I'll leave that to him, Father. He's much better at it than I am."

TWENTY

CRAIG WILHELMS'S BODY had been found in his car in the garage of his duplex in Oak Park. The ignition was on but the gas tank was empty, and nearly two days later the interior of the garage still seemed oppressive.

"Who found him?"

"The paperboy."

A kid named Wisser wearing a Cubs hat backward stood breathing through his mouth, seemingly unsure that he liked being involved in this. From time to time, he glanced toward the street. Apparently he preferred the vantage point he had.

"How come you looked into the garage?" Keegan asked.

"The door went up."

He had ridden up the drive on his bike and was about to pitch the paper at the front door when suddenly the garage door began to rise. Afraid a car would back out, he wheeled his bike along the little walk at right angles to the drive, figuring he would just put the paper in the mail slot. That's when he noticed the previous day's paper still lying on the doorstep. He waited but the car did not back out of the garage, so he rolled his bike carefully backward and looked into the garage. He saw Mr. Wilhelms at the wheel of the car. Wisser thought the man was waiting for him to go before backing out, so he waved and rode his bike down the drive. The car didn't emerge, and after he'd finished his route he came back that way to find the garage door still open and Wilhelms still behind the wheel. And he thought of yesterday's paper lying by the door. He turned in the drive and stuck his head in the garage and called. Wilhelms didn't move. The garage smelled funny.

"I went home and my mom said call the police."

"Always do what your mom says."

Wisser seemed to want more than that. Keegan took a dollar from his pocket and handed it to the kid. Wisser backed up.

"You got an extra paper?"

"There's his." He pointed toward the door.

"Good. I just bought it."

Wisser took the dollar, straightened his Cubs hat and rode down the drive, through a little group of spectators, and away.

"What do you make of the kid saying the garage door just opened?" he asked Brill, the detective who had been called to the scene.

"The remote control is not in the car."

Brill had just got out of the front seat of the car when Keegan came in from talking with Wisser. The garage door began to go down. Keegan looked at Brill.

"Who's doing that?"

"It's a test."

There was no remote control in the car but Brill had found one in the house, in the kitchen, and one of his men was across the street, using it to close the doors. In a moment they lifted again.

"What's the range of one of those?"

"That's what we're testing."

The notion that emerged was that someone parked on the street had activated the door when young Wisser went up the drive in order to draw his attention to the body. The medical examiner had been ready to give a verdict of suicide but Brill suggested he wait.

"It could have been someone who discovered the body first, of course, and didn't want to get mixed up in it." Brill's tone gave no indication of how credible he found this.

"Having taken the remote control from the car?" Keegan asked.

Brill nodded.

"How did he get into the garage to get it?"

Brill acknowledged the problem. The doors had to be closed in order for the running motor to do its damage, but if closed there was no way to open them without a remote control.

"The one from the kitchen?"

Brill turned it over in his hand, then dropped it into his jacket pocket.

"Or he could have taken the one from the car and closed the door with it from the outside."

"Before death occurred."

Thank God Cy Horvath wasn't there to witness him engaging in such speculation. It was an article of Keegan's creed that theories are the last thing you need in investigating a crime. Facts are enough. But it was the fact that the garage door had simply opened when young Wisser arrived to deliver the paper, as if someone wanted the boy to discover the body in the garage.

"Why would someone draw attention to an apparent suicide in a way that casts doubt on it being suicide?" Cy Horvath asked, when Keegan was discussing with him the finding of Craig Wilhelms's body.

"Why would anyone want to kill him?"

"Why would he want to commit suicide?"

TWO GOOD QUESTIONS even if, as Roger Dowling said, the first included the second. Horvath was off to ask about Wilhelms at EH and Keegan had gone to the noon Mass at St. Hilary's, after which, as he had hoped, he was asked to lunch at the rectory.

"I know I'm no substitute for Christopher Bourke, Marie, but I'll do my best."

"Don't speak to me of that man, Philip Keegan. The question is, will the death of his daughter bring him to his senses?"

"His wife is dropping him," Keegan said, and Marie nearly dropped the tureen of soup she was carrying from the room after ladling their bowls full. She searched Keegan's face, trying to keep from smiling.

"How do you know that?"

"Amos Cadbury filed papers this morning."

Marie gave him a disgusted look and got a new grip on the tureen. "Amos Cadbury wouldn't touch either of them with a ten-foot pole."

"Is it true, Phil?" Roger asked.

"Of course it's true," Phil said, with only half-feigned indignation. "Do I have a reputation for lying? What is this?"

Marie scooted into the kitchen with the tureen and hurried back with the casserole.

"Janet Gray is divorcing Christopher Bourke?"

"Who the hell else could she divorce?"

"I don't consider them to be married," Marie said primly.

"Maybe she feels the same way and wants out."

Marie, having served them, pulled up a chair and sat. "Father, can you imagine Amos Cadbury representing anyone in a divorce case, let alone Janet Gray?"

"It boggles the mind."

Later in the study, it was Craig Wilhelms rather than Janet Gray that Roger wanted to talk about.

"Asking why someone would want to kill Craig Wilhelms can include Craig Wilhelms as someone."

"Yeah."

"Being associated with EH is becoming dangerous to one's health." Roger Dowling puffed on his pipe.

"The daughter, Sonya. The longtime right-hand man, Wilhelms. Janet Gray bailing out."

"And Chris Bourke giving as alibi when Sonya was killed an assignation with Loraine Howells. What have you found out about EH that casts light on any of these?"

It helped to have Roger Dowling to talk to, and in this case the burden of what Phil Keegan said was that

they had thus far come up with nothing to explain the
death of Sonya, let alone that of Craig Wilhelms. They
had nothing to explain Craig's strange behavior with
Tuttle only minutes before the body of Sonya was de-
posited in Tuttle's car. Tuttle claims he had been lured
there because Craig wanted to show him where Chris
Bourke had once confined a woman named Virginia
Verona. Now a mysteriously rising garage door made
it difficult to think that Craig had killed himself.

The thought that Bourke might have killed his own
daughter when she threatened to enter the convent was
countered by the fact that Bourke had been engaged
in his favorite occupation with Loraine Howells at the
time of the girl's death.

That Craig Wilhelms might have killed her could
have been supported by his suicide, if his death could
be seen as suicide. But the rising garage door suggested that Craig Wilhelms was himself a victim.

The finding of Sonya's body in Tuttle's car when he
was lured to the warehouse by Craig made Keegan reluctant to dismiss Craig, however. Was it possible for
an electronic garage door to be activated accidentally
so that the door just happened to rise when Wisser
arrived with the paper?

Roger listened with interest as Keegan laid it all out,
but neither man said anything that cast light on the
mess.

"It's almost as if someone were deliberately mud-
dying the waters," Roger said, and sailed a smoke ring
across the room.

TWENTY-ONE

BARNEY WAS PUZZLED by the reception he received when he showed up again at the maternal manse. Now that his mother knew about Loraine, there had to be less competition from that quarter, but the memory of being locked out of the house in which he had been raised was seared into Barney's soul. He had asked for bread and been given a stone. In exile, living in squalid rooming houses or in Loop hotels that required half a dozen chains and locks and bolts on the door to give an illusion of security, he had brooded over his father and, in the time-honored tradition of the outcast, turned to religion for consolation.

One of the benefits of television was that it brought the basics to the supine viewer. Flaked out on a succession of unmade beds, fragments of take-out meals cluttering the floor around him, Barney had cast a cold eye on the evangelical fare the tube provided. In phase one, he had talked back to the preachers and recipients of miracles, the gospel singers and Bible thumpers, mocking them, making obscene noises. Phase two began when he asked himself what standard he was measuring these programs against. It occurred to him that religion had not been much of a factor in the Kaiser household. He was disposed to think that anything rejected by Mother Maud could

not be all bad. Lying abed, he began to defend the
preachers against the imagined taunts of his mother.
It felt good to champion the mocked and oppressed.
He began to feel solidarity with his brethren in the
televised ministry. They were in the same boat, these
bellowing insincere evangelists and he. If they were
insincere. He began to doubt his own doubts.

What he came to relish were the predictions of imminent wrath, divine punishment falling like fire upon
the earth. All one had to do was switch to the commercial channels to see the contrast. Violence, sex,
greed. Dante could not have portrayed the capital sins
more graphically. News programs reinforced the conviction that these were the end times. Surely God could
not long tolerate modern civilization. Barney's scruffy
exterior, the beard that looked unshaven rather than
cultivated, his billowing unclean clothes, began to
seem the costume of a prophet.

He was perfectly content at first to practice his
ministry in a horizontal position, head propped up, the
tube aglow, his prophetic brothers inveighing against
the sins and crimes of the nation. But this passivity
began to go when he happened upon the Bourkes and
watched appalled as the couple spoke with a smiling
complicity of the most intimate facts of life. Barney
had fought off advances in the men's room at the Y,
he had slunk into strange-smelling cinemas to watch
X-rated movies that had left him painfully in heat,
disgusted with himself and the world. After that, it
was no longer possible to pass women on the street
without thinking of the moaning harridans of the

pornographic screen, capable of any indignity, their genitals displayed as if for gynecological examination, the camera's eye seeking to return to the womb. There was no story in such films and Barney's thoughts were ever on the occasion of the filming, the fact that flesh-and-blood humans, real women, engaged in such antics before a camera crew. Those filmed performances sullied all women, incriminated all women, made of them unwitting accomplices in the age-old campaign to drag men about by their libidos.

Into sin. Into hellfire. Unto damnation.

He felt called to do something, something dramatic, something that would wake up even those seemingly intent on perdition. Torn between an impulsive and well-planned act, he gravitated toward the latter. Having selected his target, he moved for several weeks from sleazy hotel to sleazy hotel and, after he struck, boarded a Greyhound for Milwaukee. He checked into the Y, plugged in his television, and knew days of angry frustration. There was nothing on the news, nothing at all. In the public library on Wisconsin Avenue, in the reading room, in a Chicago paper several days old, he finally found an item. It was not much, a small story. "Suspicious Fire at Loop Porn Theater." He photocopied the story, repressing the urge to show it to others, to hint, if not say outright, that this was his handiwork. He conquered the temptation. For it was a temptation. He was embarked on the Lord's work and whatever credit he received must come from the Lord alone.

Festering in his consciousness was the realization that Loraine was involved with the ineffable Chris Bourke and his compliant wife. Loraine brought dishonor on them all. But he refused to allow the personal to distort his scale of values, God's scale of values. Loraine was far from being the prime offender. The weight of justice must fall first on the center of the enterprise.

When Loraine appeared in the public prints and on the diminutive screen of Barney's black-and-white TV, revealed at last for what he had long known she was, he found it easy to read the inner significance of the event. It was time to go home.

From the moment he walked into the house he felt closer to his mother than he ever had before, although her faults and absurdities had never been more obvious. Her life revolved around the Illinois Lottery, the track, and television game shows. Barney tried to wean her from those, but he could see the unexpected truce would quickly be broken if he insisted, so he settled for watching his own favorite fare on the little black-and-white in the room where he had spent his childhood. There were even some well-thumbed magazines far back on the top shelf of the closet, mementos of self-abuse, which he took out back and burned. He stood there with the acrid plume of smoke lifting skyward like a burnt offering to the Almighty. Barney Kaiser repents and mends his ways.

And he did. Random rancor began to give way to systematic plans of action. He got a job in a warehouse, one where his bulk was no handicap, and he bought a secondhand VW van with 90,000 miles on it, the body battered and rusty, the upholstery tattered and stained. But he was filled with the pride of ownership. He had never before owned a car. He had no driver's license, but that was no impediment to maneuvering the van out of the lot and puttering off home.

"What on earth is that?" Maud cried.

"Transportation."

"You're not going to leave it out on the street!"

He parked it in back, next to where he had burned the dirty magazines. Thank God it was spring going on summer. The van would not be much of a winter car. If winter comes. Barney's plan called for completion long before the summer season was over.

"Where are you going?" he asked Maud late one Saturday afternoon. She was all dolled up, a few spit curls emerging from her velveteen hat, purse strap lashed across her chest.

"You want to come along?"

The track? She wouldn't go dressed like that.

"Mass."

He stared at her, but she was serious. The word evoked dim memories of the time before his father was killed. His father had been Catholic, but the family connection died with him.

"You can watch Bourke on television and save yourself the trip."

"You ought to come with me."

"No church could hold me," he said, patting his belly.

But she was not disposed to have fun made of it. She stepped toward him. "There's a priest. Father Dowling. He said he'd talk with you."

"Lucky me."

"Barney, please." Her eyes left his face, then returned. "I feel responsible. You weren't raised as you should have been. As your father would have wanted. Barney, you're not even baptized." She was gripping his arm.

"There you're wrong, Mother."

Her mouth fell open. "Have you ..."

"With fire and the Holy Ghost!"

A cab stopped outside and his mother pulled open the door, urging him to come with her, but she had been taken aback by his response. He watched her go down the walk and back her butt into the opened back door of the cab. And then she was gone. To Mass. Amazing. Of course she was seventy-three and must be thinking that death was just around the corner. Suddenly he was filled with rage. Turning to God was one thing, but she should do it direct. Did she really think she had to go to a church to get through to God? He wished he had prevented her from going and talked some sense into her. If she wanted to talk about the Almighty, he could tell her a thing or two. He had felt the fire. He had felt the warm breath of the spirit pass through his soul.

TWENTY-TWO

EDDIE GOT THE MESSAGE to Bourke indirectly, as much to get a rise out of him as to fulfill the terms of the job. Any woman who asked another man to monitor her husband's movements belonged in Chaucer, not Chicago, and deserved everything she got. At the moment, a number of Bourke's overdue bills were being paid, and Eddie Hill, sitting behind the wheel of the stretch, ticked them off with satisfaction. Sonya, now Craig, public attention on a squalid little liaison with Loraine, and Janet. On a scale of aggravation, it was his wife's defection that hit Bourke the hardest.

"We switching our legal business to Amos Cadbury?" Eddie asked Bourke, directing the question over his shoulder, his eyes on the rearview mirror.

"Who's Amos Cadbury?"

Eddie laughed. He could take a joke.

"I'm serious. Who is Cadbury?"

"A lawyer."

"I've got a lawyer."

"I just wondered."

Eddie concentrated on his driving but before they had gone a block, Bourke asked, "What's this about Cadbury?"

"I thought you knew..."

"Dammit, Eddie," Bourke said menacingly.

So he told him about driving Janet to Cadbury's office. He went up with her, leaving his cap in the car, just another guy in a glen plaid suit, and when she was immediately ushered in to Cadbury, tried to engage Miss Cleary, the secretary, in conversation.

"Who are you?" she said frostily in response to his overture.

"I'm with Mrs. Bourke."

"Who is Mrs. Bourke?"

"The lady I came with."

"I have no idea who you came with, Mr.—"

"Collina," he said, using the original form out of a sudden sense of anger.

"Miss Gray?" The woman read from an appointment book, her brows lifting slowly before her eyes appeared over the rims of her glasses.

There is a gesture made with extended finger that seemed called for at the moment, but Eddie turned and left. He took compensatory satisfaction in the apparent fact that the secretary did not know who the woman was who was consulting Amos Cadbury.

In the car, exorcising the image of the bitch secretary, Eddie savored the purpose of Janet's visit to the lawyer. It was as though she had wanted him to know, babbling over the car phone to her friend Miriam. Miriam was a little gray-haired woman who wore dark-blue suits, white blouses, and a cross pinned to her lapel. Old friends. The only real friend Janet Gray had, so far as Eddie could see, and he might not have found out about her if Janet, on the way back from visiting

Sonya in Evanston, hadn't directed Eddie to the house in Winnetka.

"You needn't wait, Eddie," she said.

"No reason not to." Bourke had flown to Tokyo on R&R and at that moment some little geisha might be walking barefoot on his back.

"I'll manage. Thanks."

She was dismissing him. Eddie jotted down the address, asked around the neighborhood.

"Some sort of convent," the kid at the station told him. Eddie left the driver's door open so the kid could get a glimpse of the front of the car. Now he opened the back door, as if to inspect the passenger area. "Franciscans?" the kid said at his shoulder, gawking at the facing leather seats, the bar, the miniature television.

It turned out to be the order from which Janet Gray had departed years ago. Eddie had a lot to think about and he drove with speed and skill along Lake Shore Drive, needing the stimulus of traffic. Parked, he did not think as clearly, but give him the challenge of a hundred other vehicles whose drivers instinctively resented the appearance among them of this plutocratic machine, and Eddie's mind began to purr.

Janet had been concerned on the way to Evanston, but she came out of Sonya's place in a real snit. Then the diversion to the place in Winnetka, a convent. At first Eddie had thought Janet had forced Sonya to tell her what convent it was she meant to enter, and he smiled at the fiendishness of the girl's revenge. Enter the convent over whose walls her mother had gone before she was born. But that, amazingly, was not it. Janet had turned to the one person she trusted, Miriam Green. Sister Miriam. The nun looked her age and it was difficult to believe that these two had been contemporaries in the novitiate. Of course Janet thought the passenger area was soundproof when all this came out. Nevertheless, the third time he drove her to Winnetka, returning from a luncheon, Janet said, "Don't mention Miriam to anyone, Eddie."

He made a circle with index finger and thumb. Like Metternich or Kissinger, he would sup with any devil if the spoon was long enough.

What did it all mean? Honest to God, working for this outfit could turn you into a philosopher. Eddie was distracting himself with Mozart's Piano Concerto No. 21 when there was a tap on the window and he looked up to see a sly little face shadowed by the brim of a tweed hat pulled down low over the forehead. Eddie lowered the window.

"Good afternoon, Mr. Tuttle."

The lawyer seemed surprised to be recognized, but he recovered. "Good man. Where can we talk?"

"Get in."

Tuttle stepped back from the car, adjusted his hat, and then hurried around to the other side. Eddie hit the button, unlocking the door, and Tuttle slid in beside him. He whistled softly as he looked around. "I'll take it."

"Wanna go for a ride?"

Eddie kept within a mile of EH so that he could be back in minutes if summoned. Meanwhile Tuttle was trying the proletarian approach.

"You and I should own a car like this, Eddie."

Eddie smiled. No point in telling Tuttle the car belonged to him.

"Not that Christopher Bourke doesn't come from common origins. Before he entered the priesthood, I mean. You knew the man is an ordained priest?"

"That's what I'm told."

Tuttle shook his head. "It's hard to believe."

"What do you want, Mr. Tuttle?"

"Who killed Sonya?"

"How would I know a thing like that?"

"Aw, come on, Eddie. Who would know more than you about Christopher Bourke, his wife and child?"

"If I knew anything, I'd have to go to the police."

"I am an officer of the court, Eddie."

"I'll remember that."

"Okay then. What do you think happened to Craig Wilhelms?"

"He was killed."

Tuttle snorted. "But who did it?"

Eddie had gone through such questions with Agnes Lamb. She at least had not tried the solidarity ploy, but he had told her even less than he told Tuttle. Tuttle he told to check with Officer Lamb.

"I told her all I know."

"Then you can tell me."

"She told me to keep quiet, Tuttle," Eddie lied. "She doesn't want the case ruined."

Predictably, Tuttle squirmed in agony, wanting Eddie to divulge to him what he had allegedly already told Agnes Lamb. Eddie found being questioned easier than he would have thought. He let Tuttle out of the car a block from EH.

"I'll keep in touch," Tuttle said.

"Where can I reach you?"

Tuttle took off his hat and pulled from it what looked to be a used calling card and handed it to Eddie. "That phone's disconnected. You want me, call Peanuts Pianone."

"Who's he?"

"Just call the police and ask for Pianone."

"Agnes Lamb told me to ask for her."

Tuttle's wounded expression stayed with Eddie as he continued to his reserved parking place at EH.

TWENTY-THREE

"THE GUY WAS A CATHOLIC," Phil Keegan said, as he fell into his favorite chair in the study of the St. Hilary rectory. "Can you believe it? A convert. And then he goes on working for EH."

Craig Wilhelms was buried from the cathedral, though without fanfare, and Roger Dowling was there. He did not concelebrate but donned an alb and took a prie-dieu in the sanctuary. Even in a small church, the turnout for Craig Wilhelms would have seemed pathetically small, but in the cathedral the funeral Mass seemed merely a distraction to the dozens of visitors who came and went, doing their private devotions. Some dropped into pews and remained, but for the most part the mourners for the man whose death had been equivocal enough that no report of suicide had been made were the handful in the front pews. An aged mother, obviously unfamiliar with the ceremony but finding it no more incredible than the death of her son, sat working her mouth as if rehearsing speeches she doubted she would get to make. A sister twice the size of the mother, a brother and his diminutive wife. The only Catholic mourner was Katie Powell, kneeling erect, joined hands pressed to her lips, eyes red with tears.

Santini, the celebrant, was the priest who had admitted Craig to the Church. Iron-gray hair, the look of a man whose eye was on the next world—he was in remission from leukemia—he said the fastest Mass Roger Dowling had witnessed in years. It reminded him of the crypt at the seminary to which members of the faculty came in the morning to whisper their private Masses at the dozen altars set in alcoves along the sides of the room with its low arched ceiling. The susurrus of several Latin Masses, and in the back, just inside the doors, two confessionals where sins were whispered in English.

"He'd done a lot of reading before he came to me," Santini had said the night before, after the rosary in the funeral home. "The man was already a Catholic in his heart. Baptism of desire."

"When was that?"

Santini looked at his watch, as if he might find the answer there. "It's April," he said.

"That's right."

"A year ago. I spared him the Holy Saturday spectacle and baptized him privately. In the middle of Lent."

Santini seemed glad he had been able to give so precise an answer. He looked at Roger Dowling. "Why?"

"Do you know where he worked?"

"Something in television."

It was a mark of Santini's otherworldliness that he should have remained unaware of the circumstances of his convert's life and employment. As for suicide, he dismissed it.

"Impossible."

"That sure?"

"In a different time, the man might have become a monk, a Trappist, a Carthusian. I advised against it."

"He asked about it?"

The convert in his first fervor often wants to devote his whole life to the newfound religious belief. Roger Dowling was struck by the symmetry of the cases of Craig and Sonya Bourke, and the presence of Katie Powell at the funeral intrigued him.

"You knew him?" Santini asked, when they were on their way to the cemetery in the back seat of an official car.

"Not personally."

"Impersonally?" Santini's smile revealed a glinting gold tooth. He settled back in evident content for the rest of the ride.

Katie Powell was at graveside too and the tears flowed freely now. Roger Dowling left Santini to the grim duty of consoling the little band of relatives and caught up with Katie as she hurried toward a little Japanese car.

"Could I hitch a ride with you?" he asked.

Her expression was one of wondrous grief and she dabbed at her eyes as if to clear them.

"Father Roger Dowling," he said.

"Yes, Father. I remember. Of course I'll give you a ride."

She opened the passenger door for him and waited
to close it after he got in. Memories of another day
when the clergy were regularly deferred to came to
him, and he found that he missed that, a bit. Once she
was behind the wheel, she smiled straight ahead.

"That was like going to Sonya's funeral. I never got
to that."

"Did you know Craig Wilhelms?"

"I only met him once."

"How would you like a cup of coffee?"

She nodded with pursed lips. She wasn't through
crying yet. He suggested they go to the St. Hilary's
rectory for their coffee.

"Wouldn't it be a bother?"

"It will ensure that you take me all the way home."

Marie served them coffee in the front parlor, where
Roger Dowling got his pipe going.

"You only met him once?"

"He was a friend of Sonya's."

"A fellow convert."

"Was he a convert?"

"That's what I'm told."

"Isn't it sad, Father? First Sonya and now him. I
suppose he wasn't all that young, but Sonya . . ."

Craig Wilhelms had been forty-four years old.
"And they were friends."

She pushed her coffee cup aside and leaned toward
him. "Father, there's something I have to tell you. I
have to tell someone. Sonya went to my parents' home
in Waukegan. That's where she was hiding out when
her parents reported her missing. I promised to tell no

one where she was, and I didn't. Just Craig. But he explained to me they were friends and it seemed all right. I actually drove up there, having him follow me, so he would find the house."

"But you had met him before?"

"No, that was the only time."

"I see."

"Oh, Sonya knew him. I left as soon as I saw it was all right."

"And she was glad to see him?"

"Oh, yes. I haven't said anything about that to the police and that bothers me, I don't know why. It can't have anything to do with what happened . . ."

"What did happen?"

"Sonya was kidnapped." She looked at him as if he were senile.

"When did you last see her?"

"Then. When I brought him to Waukegan."

"Did Wilhelms say why he wanted to see her?"

"Oh, he made it clear he wasn't sent by either of Sonya's parents."

"Maybe you ought to tell the police. What harm can it do now?"

"You don't know my folks, Father."

"What a lovely girl," Marie said when Katie was gone. "Why haven't I ever met her?"

"I met her at a funeral."

He told Phil Keegan what Katie had told him and Phil frowned. "She took him to the house in Waukegan?"

"She drove ahead and he followed."

"I wonder who followed him."

Having said it, Phil didn't want to pursue the thought, but it stayed in Roger Dowling's mind and he pondered it long after Phil had gone and he sat on in the study, one lamp burning, smoking his pipe. Marie had been certain that only bad things could follow from Chris Bourke's visit to the rectory, and Roger Dowling could not help but think that it had been an odd series of events indeed that followed on the visit with the former priest. The difficulty lay in knowing whether that first visit had been prompted by what Chris told him, his daughter seeking to enter a convent.

"Sonya, in a convent?" Katie had said, when he mentioned it to her. "At first I didn't believe it. She was interested in the religious life as a phenomenon, but not for herself. The life of faith, the inner life, all that was new to her and she was fascinated. But she was going with someone . . ."

"Oh?"

"I think it must have been Craig. That's why I took him to her. I was sure he was the one she would only drop hints about. That he was older than Sonya was clear, so when Craig came and asked where she was, I just knew he was the one."

"Did you ask him?"

"As a matter of fact, I did."

"And?"

"He blushed, Father. A man that age. He was so embarrassed I was embarrassed. But he nodded."

Had Chris Bourke been lying about his daughter's intention of joining a convent? There was the note, but had Sonya written it? It was not a welcome thought, that after all these years, after the career he had made of his apostasy, Chris would look him up only to mislead and manipulate him. But what then had he wanted? Amos Cadbury's tale about Janet Gray suggested that it was his wife rather than his daughter that Chris had been concerned about. Still, Sonya had dropped out of sight, he now knew that she'd been in hiding in Waukegan, and her parents went on the air to sound the alarm. But it was Katie's revelation that Wilhelms had come to her and she had, whether wisely or not, led him to where Sonya was in hiding that filled his mind. And Phil's remark invited the thought of someone else, a third party, following the two cars to Waukegan. Had Wilhelms been a stalking horse for Christopher Bourke?

The possibility that Bourke had sought to gain his help on the basis of a lie prepared Roger Dowling to entertain the worst suspicion of the man, at least in the privacy of his own mind, sitting up late in the rectory study, puffing on his pipe as he tried to make sense of recent events. It now appeared that Chris feared the arguably more devastating desire of his wife to return to the religious life she had fled in order to become his wife and partner in EH. But this supplied no motive for him to harm his daughter—Roger Dowling kept the thought as vague as that. If anything, he would have turned on Janet. That would have been his direct recourse. But direct suggested indirect. Had Chris thought to influence his wife through their child? God knew that when the two of them appeared on television to announce her disappearance, Janet had seemed of the two more genuinely shaken by the alleged kidnapping. Perhaps Wilhelms had been performing an errand for her, going to Sonya's roommate and unexpectedly striking gold. *Sonya? She's staying in my parents' home in Waukegan.* But what then of Katie's guess that Sonya had been in love with Craig Wilhelms?

Some of these questions could be answered by putting direct questions to Chris Bourke, but Roger Dowling found himself unwilling to confront the renegade priest. Besides, it was past time that he had a talk with Janet Gray.

MAUD KAISER CAME BY, alone, without the son she had asked him to talk to. Roger Dowling had agreed, of course, but it seemed that the son was unwilling.

"Living alone has made him strange, Father." She pushed a strand of hair under the hat she wore.

"I thought he lived with you."

"Till recently he was on his own. I threw him out."

All unhappy families are alike? Barney sounded sui generis even to Roger Dowling, who had listened to his share of parental lamentations about disappointing children. But there was a grudging tone of admiration in Maud's voice.

"He's smart as a whip, Father. The way he watches television so much you wouldn't think he had time for reading, but he does. And his books!" She rolled her eyes. They were in a parlor of the rectory, where there were few books in evidence. "He believes in God but hates religion."

The priest nodded. He suspected that Barney's theological musings would be banal enough firsthand but retailed through Maud they would be more than he could bear.

"There is a lot in religion to hate, I suppose."

"The Bourkes." She leaned toward him, brows lifting. "Now them he hates the most."

"I hope he doesn't consider theirs to be a religious program."

"Oh, but he does. Is it true that man was a priest?"

Roger Dowling nodded. Was Maud as shocked as she seemed? Was her son Barney? By his mother's account he fulminated against Chris and Janet.

"But calmly now, Father. Very calmly. He is convinced that they are going to be punished."

If Barney only knew the ills currently assailing the Bourkes he might seek a different target for his anger. Their daughter dead, and perhaps by Chris's hand, at one another's throats, Janet expressing the desire to return to the convent after years and years of scandalizing believers, a divorce, Craig Wilhelms dead— what more could possibly happen to them?

"Loraine Howells is my niece. Barney's cousin."

"For heaven's sake."

"It kind of brings it home."

"No doubt."

"Oh, I wish he'd come talk to you, Father."

"I'm always here."

After she left, Roger Dowling doubted he would ever see Barney Kaiser. But he sat at his desk, pondering the odd fact that this woman who had dropped out of the blue was related to the more lurid events that had been occupying him for some time. The image of the overweight son carrying on arguments with his little television set in an upstairs room that had been his when he was a boy, wishing the wrath of God on the Bourkes, was an arresting one. It was like hearing that someone somewhere was sticking pins in effigies of the famous television twosome.

TWENTY-FOUR

TUTTLE SAT BEHIND the wheel of the Toyota, slumped down, hat lowered over his eyes, his gaze upon the stretch.

"I hate those windows," he said to Peanuts, who sat beside him munching on a Big Mac. It sounded as if he were eating the polystyrene container as well as the burger. "I know he's in there, but I can't see him."

"He can see us," Peanuts said.

True enough but what was there to see? Eddie Hill was in there, comfortable in his leather seat, reading a book. He really did read, it wasn't a prop. Tuttle had gone over the stretch pretty thoroughly, thanks to Peanuts's ability to open any locked car door in fifteen seconds.

"Thank God you're honest," Tuttle said. And when Peanuts did not understand, "I can see that any car can be stolen, locked or not."

"You're safe with this one."

"Thanks a lot." The Toyota was paid for and Tuttle never worried about scratches or bending a fender. Nothing could hurt his battered vehicle and it was a liberating thought. Imagine the anxiety Eddie must feel wheeling that monster of a limo around. Tuttle noticed the care with which Eddie parked the car and never in a lot where an opening door on an adjacent car could leave its signature on the gleaming stretch.

"Nothing on this guy Hill, Peanuts?"

Peanuts shook his head.

"You looked?"

"I asked Agnes Lamb to do it." Peanuts smiled smugly.

"You what!" Tuttle had stared in disbelief at Peanuts.

"She's good at it," Peanuts said grudgingly, put back by Tuttle's reaction.

"What reason did you give her?"

"That I was busy."

"I mean what reason did you give her for running a check on Eddie Hill?"

Peanuts thought about it. "She didn't ask for any."

"Just said she'd do it."

"Yeah."

"What a dumb thing to do!"

Peanuts's narrow eyes narrowed further. He was sensitive to remarks about his mental capacities. Tuttle realized he had gone too far. He could not afford to alienate Peanuts Pianone. He put his hand on his friend's arm.

"I shouldn't have asked you to do it."

Only maybe it hadn't been so dumb. Agnes had had a talk with Eddie, and now here they were waiting to see what the chauffeur's reaction would be. Tuttle, slumping back out of sight, felt edgy. This stakeout to keep an eye on Eddie Hill was private enterprise. He had mounted what he liked to think of as a rival investigation to the official one, insofar as there was an official one. Agnes Lamb was going by the numbers, if Peanuts could be believed, dutifully interviewing everyone at EH in exhaustive recorded sessions. Of course she would have to prepare a digest. Plunking down hundreds of pages of testimony on Phil Keegan's desk was an unwise thing to do. Tuttle was keeping what he had learned in his head, though much of it was what he knew of the investigation from Peanuts. That was why he knew that they hadn't considered the EH chauffeur to be an important figure in events. Tuttle knew otherwise.

When he and Peanuts went through the stretch last night in the rental garage downtown where Eddie left the car when he was off, they had come upon the chauffeur's recording system. Although Eddie owned the limo, it would have been possible to think that the audio- and videotaping equipment of the passenger compartment was something Christopher Bourke had persuaded Eddie to install, but from the copies Tuttle had made of the audiotapes, it seemed unlikely that Bourke had instructed Eddie to keep the tape running; unlikely, but not impossible. Maybe like the Watergate tapes, the one who authorized them forgot they had been installed and were constantly running. But no such forgetfulness was possible on the part of the operator. The tape in the limo persuaded Tuttle that he and Peanuts would have to take a look into Eddie's apartment. In a basement workroom, they found the cache of tapes, along with duplicating capacity. Over the course of several days, Tuttle made duplicates of all the audiotapes. They provided him with a record of conversations that had taken place in the passenger compartment over a two-year period. Tuttle had fallen asleep and come awake with the voices of Bourke, Janet Gray, and others humming in his ears. It seemed inescapable now that the police would eventually come into possession of those tapes. Unless Eddie, alerted by Agnes's visit, did something first. Destroy them? He hadn't recorded all that back-seat action in order to throw it all away, which was why he and Peanuts were parked here waiting for Eddie to make a move. Tuttle had thought he had all the time in the world to try to make sense out of what he had learned. Now the clock was running. If Tuttle was to come up with the big answer before the police and somehow profit from that knowledge, he was going to have to hurry. Tuttle had come to know that Agnes Lamb had an uncanny nose for criminal activity among the white folk, and he doubted Eddie would be able to deflect her for long.

Sitting there, they had seen Agnes come and go. Eddie was parked up the street, behind the opaque windows of the limo, and they were waiting for him to do something.

The limo began to move away so slowly that at first Tuttle thought it was an illusion created by prolonged concentration on an immobile object. He turned the ignition key as he sat up, but in his eagerness he ground the starter and failed to start the engine. He got it on the second try and woke up Peanuts.

"He's leaving!" Tuttle cried.

"Big deal," grumbled Peanuts.

"This is what we've been waiting for."

"We." Peanuts made a farting sound with his lips.

Tuttle ignored him. He had flushed his bird and now took aim on the rapidly accelerating limo. Had Eddie waited so long after the interview with Agnes in order to make sure he was not under surveillance? Tuttle felt invisible in the battered Toyota. Only a paranoid Eddie would imagine that Tuttle's wreck of a car could belong to the police.

If Tuttle had driven directly to Eddie's apartment they would have arrived before the limo. Eddie took a very circuitous route and Tuttle hung back, trying to lose himself in traffic, lest Eddie notice the Toyota. When it became clear where Eddie was headed, Tuttle banked off and approached the apartment from the opposite direction, parking half a block away, with the underground garage entrance in view.

"Now what?"

"Let's wait awhile."

"Before what?"

Good question and one best left unanswered.

In any case, the nose of the limo emerged from the garage fifteen minutes after entering and turned to come toward Tuttle's Toyota. From the front, Eddie was visible behind the wheel and Tuttle sat frozen, unable to duck out of sight, certain that Eddie would notice the car, their eyes would meet, the whole stake-out rendered useless. But Eddie went by staring intently into the rearview mirror. After he passed, Tuttle did slide down, tugging his tweed hat from his head.

Peanuts just sat there but maybe that was an advantage. Eddie wouldn't recognize Peanuts. Then Tuttle started the Toyota, made a U-turn, and followed Eddie at a safe distance.

Tuttle didn't know what to make of it when Eddie pulled over to the curb at the Union Station. It came as a surprise to find that trains still ran, although traffic was nothing like what it had once been. Eddie carried a medium-sized sports bag slung over his shoulder, and it bounced off his hip as he walked. He seemed to be making an effort to look nonchalant.

Peanuts came along, although Tuttle just slid out of the car and went after Eddie without saying a word.

"I ain't been here in years," Peanuts said.

Eddie never looked back after he went into the station. Tuttle pulled Peanuts out of sight and they watched Eddie go to the luggage check and slide the sports bag over the counter. Tuttle would bet his bottom dollar that the bag contained Eddie's supply of audiotapes. Good man. This would keep them out of Agnes's grasp.

They moved around the pillar when Eddie returned.

"We going?" Peanuts asked.

"Mission accomplished, Peanuts."

"Thanks for distracting him, Pianone."

Tuttle wheeled around to face Agnes Lamb and a uniformed officer he did not recognize.

"You're welcome," Peanuts said, obviously confused.

"This the way you spend your off-duty, playing cop?"

"I'm helping Tuttle."

"And me. Let's go see what's in the bag, shall we?"

Tuttle felt sick. An afternoon of effort was wasted and he stood there trying not to cry. But he and Peanuts went with Agnes and Officer Anzac to the luggage counter, where Agnes flashed her badge and the attendant made routine protests that were partly overridden when Peanuts too showed his shield.

"Get the goddamn sports bag," Anzac said. He looked like an altar boy but his tone was that of a hit man. The attendant got the bag. Agnes unzipped it and removed a cassette. She looked quizzically at Tuttle but he shrugged his shoulders.

"Well, I gotta get going," Tuttle said. "Coming with me, Peanuts?"

"Hell yes."

Was Agnes smiling triumphantly after them? Did Anzac wonder what he and Peanuts had been doing? Does the bear sleep in the woods?

"I'm hungry," Peanuts said when they came outside.

TWENTY-FIVE

EDDIE HILL WAS OBVIOUSLY an educated man, but any question as to why he had settled for employment as a chauffeur seemed to be answered by the tapes. He had rigged the passenger compartment so that he was always privy to what was going on and could record any sessions of special interest. Cy and Keegan and Agnes had listened to samples of seductions, business schemes, more seductions, and puzzling conversations between Janet Gray and a woman named Miriam.

"Of course we can't use them," Arvin Straddle from the prosecutor's office said, holding up a hand as if a line of schoolchildren were about to troop through his office.

"They weren't taken from his home," Agnes said.

That didn't matter to Straddle. He was new, a year or two out of law school, and saw his function as one of restraining the repressive police and protecting the threatened rights of citizens. Cy had accompanied Agnes to the prosecutor's office and was not at all surprised. So they trooped back to Keegan's with their inadmissible evidence.

"So what?" Keegan asked. "We now know a lot more about their operation than we did before."

"Straddle says we have to return them to Eddie Hill."

"Of course. I understand copying tapes is a comparatively simple process."

"Should I . . ."

It was Keegan's turn to hold up his hands as he continued to address the world at large. "The originals of course must be returned to their rightful owner."

Agnes saw his point and stopped seeking further clarification. Cy had listened to all the tapes, or at least to sufficient samples, before he sat down with Eddie Hill.

"You're an educated man," Cy said.

"Self-educated."

"Not all chauffeurs are."

"It gives me a chance to read."

"You have a curious mind."

Hill glanced at him. "My lawyer assures me you can do absolutely nothing with those tapes."

"Who's your lawyer?"

"A man named Tuttle."

Did Hill know that Tuttle and Peanuts had been following him around, providing Agnes with a convenient cover? Good old Tuttle. Eddie Hill had the lawyer he deserved.

"He's absolutely right."

Eddie folded his arms and sat back, relieved. Perhaps he already suspected that Tuttle had not graduated at the head of his class.

"Who is Miriam?"

"Miriam?"

"The friend of Mrs. Bourke's."

"Just that. A friend of hers."

"Where does she live?"

"Isn't this a question you should put to Janet?"

"Do you call your employers by their Christian names?"

"Given names. They repudiated Christianity."

"You're sure of that?"

"What do you mean?"

"Given names, then. You call them Chris and Janet?"

"Lieutenant, they hire me and my car. I am under exclusive contract to them. But I am an independent businessman, not a servant. I consider myself no more the social inferior of my passengers than an airline pilot feels inferior to his. He probably earns more than most of them. Of course I can't say the same of myself and the Bourkes."

Sunlight glancing from the window made the blond stubble on Eddie's cheeks visible.

"Is taping their conversations one of the services you provide those who hire you?"

"I thought we agreed you can't use those."

"In court. They've given us some interesting leads. Tell me, Eddie, what did you have against Sonya and Craig?"

"I don't know what you mean."

"Where did you get the hat pin?"

Eddie crossed his legs and recrossed his arms, a fortress under siege. "What are you getting at?"

"I think you know."

"Tell me."

"I'd rather have you tell me why you opened Wilhelms's garage door when the paperboy came."

Cy Horvath had been at his work for many years, but he could not read Eddie Hill. The man's wariness and alarm when he saw the point of the questions was expected, but Cy also had the feeling that he was engaged in a game with the chauffeur, and that Eddie was listening carefully to discern if Cy would hit on the right tack to take. Animal, vegetable, mineral. Agnes spelled him and sometimes they worked together, but Eddie strengthened under the pressure and after a while seemed to be enjoying it. Why shouldn't he? He was giving them nothing. Cy took a break in Phil's office.

"I don't know."

"Nothing like a hat pin has been turned up at his place. Not that that matters."

"I think we ought to bring a charge," said Cy.

"What about Straddle?"

"He unearthed a case in which a judge found against someone for taping conversations without the consent of the speakers. It's a federal offense, so we can bypass Straddle."

"You want to go ahead on that basis?"

"I think we have to do something. This is something."

"But you don't think he's the one?"

"I wouldn't exclude it," said Cy.

Who would? Eddie might have provided an alibi for Bourke when he dropped him and Loraine off at her aunt's house for an afternoon of hanky-panky, but that left Eddie free during the crucial time when Sonya was killed. Cy wanted that limo impounded and gone over thoroughly. The trunk was more than commodious enough to carry a body, and Eddie would have been able to follow Craig to the warehouse and do the number on Tuttle. It seemed fated that Eddie would end up with Tuttle as his lawyer. How Peanuts could have missed seeing the stretch limo was not the problem it seemed, when you considered where Tuttle had parked his Toyota. No one at EH was using the limo when Craig's garage door went up as young Wisser arrived with the *Fox River Tribune,* and there was opportunity during the previous night for Eddie to be there when an unconscious Craig was propped up behind the wheel of his running car in the closed garage.

Motive?

The taping made it clear that Eddie Hill hoped to get a lot more out of his contract with EH than his fee. It was Agnes who turned up the interesting bit of tape of Sonya's voice.

"'Eddie! What are you taping?'"

"'I'm rewinding.'"

"'You are not. You can hear us back here, can't you?'"

Sonya, it appeared, had discovered Eddie's little secret. At the time she had been in the back with Katie Powell. Cy and Agnes went together to Evanston.

AGNES SAT NEXT TO KATIE on the couch, but Cy remained on his feet.

"Who else besides Craig Wilhelms knew of Sonya's staying with your parents?"

"Oh, my parents weren't here. The house was closed. They're still in Florida."

Agnes nodded. Of course. Wasn't everyone in Florida for the winter?

"And I didn't tell anyone else. I'm sure it was all right to tell Craig."

They let her tell everything she had been wanting to tell about her roommate before asking any questions about Eddie Hill.

"Would you like a Coke?" Katie asked and Agnes accepted. The girl looked at Cy.

"Do you have coffee?"

"Instant?"

"Sure." But he must have made a face the way Agnes looked at him.

"I'm so glad I have finally told you all these things."

"Better late than never," Cy said.

"Father Dowling told me I have to tell you."

Agnes said, "Let me ask you about Eddie Hill."

Katie looked back and forth between them. "Who is Eddie Hill?"

"The chauffeur of a limousine that was under contract to EH."

Katie remembered now.

"Do you have a cassette tape player?"

"I've got a Third World briefcase," Katie said to Agnes, and then turned scarlet, thinking the black officer would take offense. "I'll get it."

"What's a Third World briefcase?" Agnes whispered.

"Let's wait and see."

Katie returned with the portable tape player and Agnes took over, getting out the cassette and slipping it into place. Moments later the voices of Sonya and Katie filled the room. Katie gasped at the sound of her dead roommate's voice and put a hand over her mouth. There was something eerie about those two carefree girlish voices chattering away about classes and friends, but almost immediately the voice of Sonya was heard addressing Eddie Hill.

"Remember that?" Agnes asked.

"It was so funny. Sonya thought the passenger compartment was private, and all along Eddie was listening in. And taping. I suppose it was rigged up by her father, but Sonya was convinced it was meant to spy on her. Isn't it silly, wanting a record of a conversation like that?" She paused. "I would like a copy of it, though. Is that morbid?"

"Have you got a blank cassette?" Agnes didn't hesitate.

The portable had two drives and in a matter of minutes Katie had her copy of that pointless yet now precious conversation. Neither Cy nor Agnes told the girl that Eddie had taped all kinds of other conversations.

"Anything ever come of that episode?" Cy asked.

"What do you mean?"

"I don't know. Did Sonya mention Eddie and his taping, anything about it at all?"

"No."

"Did you ever ride in the limo again?"

"The only reason we did that time was because Sonya's father had sent for her. That's why she thought it was an effort to spy on her."

"Why?"

A sad smile came over the girl's face. "She thought she wanted to enter the convent."

Agnes sat back. "The daughter of those two wanted to enter a convent?"

"I don't know if she was serious. She was serious about her new religion. But at least at first, talk about the convent was just a way of teasing her parents. She had a very strange relationship with her parents. Her mother had said several times in public that she would have gotten an abortion if that had been possible when she was carrying Sonya. Isn't that awful? I suppose that would make you feel differently about your mother."

"Did you ever meet her, the mother?"

"No."

"Who do you think killed Sonya?"

The direct question affected her oddly. She put down her Coke, then picked it up again. "I thank God it couldn't have been Craig Wilhelms. What if I had led a man to Sonya who intended to kiss her? When I heard he was dead, well, I almost felt relief."

"Because it wasn't suicide?"

She looked wide-eyed at Agnes. "It wasn't suicide, was it?"

"The coroner says no."

"Why do you put it like that?"

"Someone made it look like a suicide and then made sure no one would think so."

Agnes shouldn't have brought it up. The girl wanted all the details. While they talked, Cy called in.

"Cy!" Keegan cried. "Thank God you called. Get back here as quick as you can."

"What's going on?"

"Chris Bourke has confessed to killing his daughter and Craig Wilhelms."

TWENTY-SIX

STILL PHOTOGRAPHS can be airbrushed and film softened with filters, reality improved by art. On the set, with makeup, lighting, and above all his persuasive tone, Chris seemed the epitome of what he preached. In bed he was something else. Loraine lay beside her exhausted lover, studying the pores in his face, the lines, the sag of flesh that made the lines of his jaw less distinct. His eyes opened and looked into hers.

"I fell asleep."

The pillow rustled in her ear when she nodded. She hated loving him, because this was all it meant, a few moments in bed, and less and less often now. Aunt Maud's was out now, of course, but he would not go to her apartment or take her to his home. Their home. His and Janet's. Their lovemaking had begun on the assumption that she accepted his philosophy of EH. If she ever had, she had rejected it now.

"What time is it?"

"Not yet three."

He sighed and closed his eyes and soon he was asleep again. Afternoon sun came through the slanted blinds of the motel window. How vulnerable he was, asleep, looking his age, his breath wheezing and whistling, the real Christopher Bourke.

If she loved him it was because she could not accept that he really thought of their times together simply as recreation, as if she were one of those inflatable dolls that had formed the subject of a recent show, surrogate sexual partners for the lonely. How pathetic they were, yet Chris and Janet had gushed over them as if they were the answer to a bachelor's prayer. Did either of them believe a word they said? Viewers would swear they were still in love, but Loraine knew the intensity of their mutual dislike as soon as the cameras were off and the lights went down. Whatever their relation had been, it had become a business one. And now Janet threatened to leave.

"You don't need her, Chris."

"It's the audience that needs her. Us. The two of us together."

"You're the attraction. Anyone could do what she does."

He tipped his head. "You?"

"I'm not photogenic."

He looked at her in an appraising way, turned back the sheet to see the rest of her. "We could find out."

But she moved tightly against him. If Janet had brains she could bring the whole organization down and depart from the shambles, but she had never understood the business side. Neither did Chris if the truth were known, but at least he made an effort. Now, studying him asleep, Loraine considered how she could ruin him if she wanted to. A really good accountant can be bad on purpose...

Such thoughts sprang from her feeling of being used by him, but what complaint did she really have? He treated her exactly as he said women wished to be treated, making no claims, permitting her to use him as he used her, the pleasure they shared self-contained, making no claims on the future.

When they had used Maud's house, she had entertained him with word pictures of her aunt, the merry widow who spent whole days at the track, gambling, buying tickets in the lottery.

"Does she ever win?"

"Not big. It's the risk she likes."

"She has learned the secret of life."

She could almost envy Maud her anonymous, predictable life, her narrow brick house, her bridge and bingo and all the rest. Well, not all the rest. The rest included Barney.

It was bad enough accepting that she was related to Maud, but Barney? Her cousin had been a lard ass as a kid, apparently smart, but that hadn't made up for his overall ugliness. She had done him a favor, though, he had moved back with his mother after the publicity. Was he grateful?

Loraine closed her eyes. It would be nice if they were to die like this, be found together, lying side by side, lovers on a Grecian urn. Chris spoke of sex as the little death, a description no doubt stolen from someone, so why couldn't it be the big death too? Such morbid thoughts made her shiver, and soon she was shaking from head to foot in a way that frightened her. She grabbed fistfuls of blanket and tried to draw them more tightly about her. Her teeth were chattering. What was happening to her?

After a moment she gained control of herself and lay staring at the blades of the blind. Beside her Chris began to snore.

TWENTY-SEVEN

CHRISTOPHER BOURKE was in a cheerful mood when he stopped by the St. Hilary rectory on his way from court where bail had been set and the self-confessed multiple murderer released. Roger Dowling knew how disgusted Phil was that Straddle had bound Bourke over despite the high unlikelihood that he could have done what he claimed to have done. Loraine Howells had provided an alibi for him covering the presumed time when Sonya was murdered, and it was doubtful, given his schedule, that Bourke could have had anything to do with Craig Wilhelms's death. So much of what he broadcast was taped in advance that it had to be established whether Bourke had been on live or taped at the crucial time, perhaps, but Bourke's manner would have removed any doubt Roger Dowling had.

"I hope you have a good reason for making these gruesome claims, Chris. Not that I can think of anything that could serve as sufficient reason."

"Preserving my marriage? Look, could we close this door?"

Roger Dowling closed the study door and Bourke drew from the inside pocket of his jacket the kind of silver cigarette case Roger Dowling had not seen in years and took out an oval Dunhill before offering the case to Father Dowling.

"I'll stay with this," the pastor said, gesturing with his pipe.

"How puritanical we have all become, Roger. Here I am, a grown man, forced to sneak a cigarette. It serves me right, of course; I have campaigned unctuously against the wicked weed for years."

"And gone on smoking?"

"The flesh is weak." Bourke tipped back his head and directed exhaled smoke at a copy of Merkelbach's *Theologia Moralis* on the shelf.

"And the spirit is nonexistent."

"Touché. Roger, I hesitate to call what I am about to say a confession, but I feel I owe you an explanation. A number of things have happened over the past year that have pretty effectively turned me on my head. The first was Janet's claim that Sonya is not my child." He paused, contemplating the burning end of his cigarette. "She made this claim during one of the arguments which, you will not be surprised to learn, are a regular feature of marital bliss. But Janet and I have turned ourselves into Siamese twins, become a single persona. What was that Shaw called Belloc and Chesterton?"

"The Chesterbelloc."

"Yes." He smiled. "We are the Janopher or perhaps the Chrisnet. So we have stuck together through thick and thin for quite frankly commercial reasons. A year ago Janet began to experience headaches of a horrendous sort. Our first fear was that she had developed a tumor. Perhaps if they had found something organically wrong, things would have been different. In any case, she was soon in the grips of the fear of death." His eyes met Roger Dowling's and their expression canceled the forced merriment of his smile. "Her thoughts turned to the Four Last Things."

"To God."

He stubbed out his cigarette and immediately his hand went to the inside pocket of his jacket, but he checked the motion. "Soon she was riddled with feelings of guilt. For years the two of us had explained such fear and guilt away. You would have thought that she of all people would have been prepared for them. But she was experiencing excruciating headaches for which there was no natural cause. Of course she began to think of them as punishment."

"Are you saying her faith returned?"

"You would put it that way, of course. For the better part of a year the Janet people see on television is a Janet who is no more. Everything involving her is a rerun. The day came when she linked her headaches to the continued showing of those programs. The sight of herself urging others to throw off their chains and enjoy life intensified her fear and guilt. She wanted out."

"Would that really be so devastating?"

"She looked up a member of her old community. Roger, when I first came to you, it was a ruse. I spoke of my daughter, but of course I was thinking of Janet. She had disappeared and I had every reason to think she had gone into retreat at some convent."

"I understand she is seeking a divorce."

"That is part of it, yes."

"So you killed your daughter..."

"If she was my daughter."

"And Craig Wilhelms as well as Sonya?"

"Sonya to shake Janet out of it, Craig because he knew too much."

"That doesn't make any sense at all, you know."

"Oh, I don't know."

"Chris, what are you trying to accomplish? Whoever did kill those two—"

"Janet did."

"What?"

"This is in total confidence. You would have had to see the changes in her during these past months. Sonya came to represent for her a sin that had to be expiated. And it was her sin alone. She insisted on that when I told her I would carry whatever guilt she thought was attached to our daughter. She informed me that Sonya was not my daughter, that she had in effect seduced me in order to have a father for her child. She was weighed down by what she had done. The solution was to offer Sonya in sacrifice, as expiation for her sins."

Was he serious even now? Roger Dowling found it impossible to tell. The man had spent a lifetime in subterfuge and deception. Perhaps anyone might devote himself pell-mell to the pursuit of pleasure, first a victim of weakness and then of habit, but Christopher Bourke had become an apostle of hedonism, it was a theoretical thing with him, and he had used it to enrich himself. He might have done the same thing with the gospel, but thank God he had not. Of course that was a crowded field. But Roger Dowling suspected that Chris was as cynical about the panacea of sex as many television evangelists were about their message. Finally, the message was the medium, a means of amassing wealth. By his own admission, Chris had come to him before with a lie on his lips. How could Roger know that this time the man was telling the truth?

"Why kill Craig Wilhelms?"

"More guilt. They'd had an affair that was the destruction of his marriage. A good marriage, as you would say. How could she return to religion with a daughter conceived in sin and a lover whose life she had ruined out there as living rebukes to her pretensions? Both had to be removed."

"She said this?"

"I know her as well as I know myself."

Roger Dowling did not consider this a large claim. One who deceives others must first deceive himself.

"How is your confessing to such crimes meant to address these matters?"

"Gallantry is not dead, Roger. She may repudiate me, but I will not repudiate her. Call it a natural-law case for marital fidelity. She is my wife. I will shoulder the burden of her guilt."

That was when Roger was certain Chris was lying, but which lie was the important one? His portrayal of himself as the self-sacrificing spouse did not ring true, but was he also lying about Janet? If Phil was right, no case worth speaking of could be made against Chris, no matter how many times he confessed. That meant that charges would be dropped and of course the media could be informed about Chris's motivation. This would have the double effect of saving him as a cult figure and of directing suspicion at Janet, whether or not she was truly guilty. It looked as if Chris Bourke was continuing to manipulate events for his own purposes. If so, nothing had changed since his first visit.

"Very interesting," Roger said, knocking the ashes from his pipe. "But I have to say the noon Mass."

"You don't believe me."

"I am not the one you have to convince."

"I wanted you to know." He stood and patted his chest. Roger Dowling feared he was going to swear to the veracity of his story, but he was merely checking his cigarette case. "I felt I owed you an explanation."

Roger let Chris out and came down the hallway. Marie Murkin sped past him with lowered head, her manner suggesting that she thought it would be a good idea to bell, book, and candle the house after the third visit from the apostate priest. Roger Dowling wasn't sure he didn't agree with her.

"MAYBE IF YOU'D CALL HIM," Maud Kaiser said, having apologized for her son, Barney, who had not yet come to see Father Dowling.

"I wouldn't push it too hard, Maud."

"You could call him at work. The way he describes the job, all he does is sit all day."

"Is he a guard?"

Maud shook her head. She had been drawn to St. Hilary's for Bingo Night at the Senior Center and, genuine as her concern for her son might be, she kept looking toward the tables, obviously anxious to get started.

"Not exactly, but sort of. It's a warehouse."

"You probably want to get a card, Maud."

She had her purse open but what she took from it was a slip of paper, which she pressed on him. "That's his number at work, Father."

And then she was off to a table and several hours of bingo.

TWENTY-EIGHT

"HE'S LYING, of course."

"Why would he do that?" Amos Cadbury asked. The Janet Gray who sat in his office for the second time bore little resemblance to the television personage that Amos, almost despite himself, had watched from time to time. The skin of her face was tight, the result, according to his secretary, of cosmetic surgery, but the hair was still the magnificent gray that had been her trademark.

"It's why I continue to use my maiden name," she said ruefully. "In religion I was Sister Mary Chrysostom."

Decades in the practice of law enabled Amos to nod almost noncommittally at this information. It was her first overt reference to her past as a nun.

"It's something you never forget. Whether I wanted to or not, I always remembered the day of my profession, the day I entered, special feast days of the order. I suppose everyone has his own private liturgy."

Amos thus remembered his wedding day, the day he had passed the bar, the day he had been named a Knight of Saint Gregory.

"Why would your husband accuse himself of such dreadful crimes?"

"To turn suspicion to me."

"I don't understand."

"Chris is always difficult to understand."

"Most people would think he is acting to protect his wife."

"I am not his wife. I thought we were agreed on that."

It was after he spoke to Roger Dowling that Amos had agreed to represent Janet Gray, explaining to her that, while technically it would be considered a divorce case, he himself did not so regard it, because she had not been canonically capable of contracting a marriage when she went through the civil ceremony. Once the divorce was obtained, her problem would be one of reinstatement rather than annulment. Roger Dowling had pressed him as to the sincerity of Janet Gray's intentions and Amos found himself unable to settle the matter with any confidence. She had the look of a penitent. She no longer went to lengths of time and expense to nullify the effects of age, she seemed genuinely anxious to be severed from Christopher Bourke, she had made contact with her old order.

"Why would your husband's confessing to two gruesome murders direct suspicion on you?"

"Because it will be easily discovered that he could not possibly have done those terrible things."

"That is a far cry from suggesting that you did them."

"Let me tell you about Christopher Bourke."

Amos Cadbury listened but he did not understand. If anything, matters became more obscure as a result of Janet Gray's attempt to clarify them. In a long and

distinguished legal career, Amos Cadbury had dealt
with a wide spectrum of human beings, from the most
innocently naive to the most cunning and devious. But
listening to Janet Gray suggested to him that there
were depths beneath what he had hitherto thought to
be the depth of human perversity. Janet's distaste and
contempt for the man with whom she had been living
for twenty years and more was palpable, and she described him as regarding her with equal contempt.
That she found the thought that he would contrive to
have her accused of the murder of her own daughter
credible tended to eclipse the suggestion that Bourke
was treating the system of justice as a manipulable toy.
To confess to two murders plausibly enough to convince a cautious soul like Arvin Straddle that an indictment was feasible was one thing; to deliberately
make a mockery of the law to which Amos Cadbury
had dedicated his life was an outrage. Amos scarcely
knew what to make of all this, and when he reminded
himself that this woman had once been a nun, that she
had subsequently spent several decades in tandem with
one of the Church's most unrelenting foes and that he
was now representing her in a divorce action, he wondered where it would all end. Had Roger Dowling any
idea of how complicated a situation this was when he
assured him that it would not really be an exception to
his clean record in leaving divorce cases alone? Amos
had the sinking feeling that whatever it was Christopher Bourke had in mind would soon involve him and
the law firm whose good name was as important to
him as his own, indeed was indistinguishable from it.

"Have you spoken with a canon lawyer?"

"Not yet. What Chris is up to, of course, is to make it all but impossible for me to be accepted back into my community. I already qualify as a public sinner, of course, but to be branded as a murderer of my own child..." Her voice trailed away as her eyes drifted to the window and filled with tears.

"And Craig Wilhelms?"

"Oh, he was my lover."

"I see."

She turned to him. "No, you don't see, Mr. Cadbury. In recent months I have gone some way toward regaining the conscience I have dulled over these years and I know what all this must seem to you. If I live to be a hundred I can never do penance enough for what I've been."

"Who killed your daughter?"

Amos surprised himself by asking the question. It was the kind of information a lawyer was better off not having.

"I don't know." She looked at him. "You expect me to say he did it, but I can't believe that. Oh, I'd like to. God knows he's capable of anything. I can imagine him killing Craig, but not Sonya. The fact that he confessed to doing those crimes almost convinces me he is innocent."

Amos was glad when the session was over. Alone he sat at his desk, palms pressed flat to its surface, and stared at the photograph of his wife on the wall. When he asked Janet if she had consulted a canon lawyer it was with the idea of bringing Roger Dowling into the case in an official capacity.

"I WILL ADVISE YOU, Amos, but that's as far as I will go."

"Would you talk with her?"

"What would be served by that?"

"I would find it helpful if I could compare notes with someone I trust."

"Notes?"

"Impressions of her. Father Dowling, I have never met such a person in all my professional career."

He found it impossible to explain what he meant to the priest but that only underscored how baffled he was by the client he had all but unwillingly taken on. Already it seemed lightyears since he had presumed to show up at the St. Hilary rectory with his strange new client in tow.

"Tell me, Amos, what has she told you of her daughter?"

"Father, I am happy to report that she is genuinely affected by the death of the girl. In almost all else, her attitude is curiously dissociated. No one detests more than I do obscuring the law with pop psychological interpretations of human acts, but this woman fairly cries out for analysis."

"Has she ever said anything about the girl's parentage?"

"I don't understand."

"Has she ever raised the question of the girl's father?"

"Christopher Bourke?"

"I think you are answering my question."

"Please, Father Dowling, not you. I came here longing for an unambiguous conversation."

"Bourke claims she told him he is not the girl's father."

"Dear God."

The tobacco smoke, strong coffee, and Marie Murkin made visits to the St. Hilary rectory punitive, but it was not these that weighed on Amos Cadbury now.

"I feel I have entered a maze, Father, and one from which I shall not emerge unscathed."

"I would have thought all these troubles would have brought them closer together."

"Theirs seems always to have been an alliance rather than a marriage, a co-conspiracy."

"It could be important to know if Christopher was not the father of Sonya."

"It is such an outrage that the prosecutor colludes with that man in this abuse of the courts."

"Who knows, maybe the indictment will stick and he'll be found guilty."

"If you would pray for that, I would be most grateful, Father."

"I will pray that justice is done. And mercy."

"Yes."

Amos sat for a moment behind the wheel of his car, waiting for the air conditioning to take hold. Strains of Gregorian chant poured from the speakers. Chants and jazz of the twenties and thirties soothed such savage breast as Amos Cadbury had. He was adjusting

the sound when he noticed a very fat young man
dressed in a wrinkled seersucker suit rolling up the
walk to the rectory door. Poor Father Dowling.
Doubtless that man was bringing him another tale of
woe. Amos put the car in drive and pulled away.

TWENTY-NINE

KEEGAN DID NOT RECOGNIZE Tuttle without the tweed hat, and the lawyer seemed to be wearing a new suit as well. Apparently representing Eddie Hill had brought a species of prosperity to Tuttle & Tuttle. And Tuttle had been consulted by Christopher Bourke's lawyers. The lawyer dropped a spanking-new business card on Keegan's desk, with the suggestion that Keegan might want to mention the man who had handled the Bourke case to unrepresented wretches who fell afoul of the law.

"Have we formally removed you from suspicion, Tuttle?"

The lawyer's reddish hair lay tousled on his round head. He smiled at Keegan. "Nice try, Captain. Perhaps you noticed that the *Tribune* gave me credit for leading you to the body of Sonya Bourke."

"Leading us to the back seat of your car, you mean. Bourke is out on bail?"

"The indictment is ridiculous. I am preparing a timetable that will demonstrate beyond the possibility of reasonable doubt that he could not have been involved in those murders."

"Tell him, not me. He's the one who insists he's guilty."

Tuttle put on a wistful smile. "What is it, Keegan? His years in the priesthood, years spent trying to help people overcome their fears and anxieties? How many men would put themselves on the block for their wives in the way he has?"

"I don't follow you."

Tuttle pulled up a chair, unzipped, zipped, then unzipped again the briefcase on his lap. He took from it the tweed hat and put it on. "My thinking cap. This is just between us, Captain, though you may choose to act on it in an official capacity and that's perfectly all right with me. The reason Bourke says he did those things is because he thinks his wife did."

"Tuttle, she's talking divorce."

The lawyer opened his hands, as if Keegan were making his case for him. "Gratitude. Hell hath no fury like a woman helped. His self-sacrifice is too much for her."

"Where did you get this bullshit, Tuttle?"

Tuttle took off his hat and returned it to his briefcase, mussed up his hair a bit and stood. He winked at Keegan. "A word to the wise."

And he was gone. Keegan buzzed Cy and Agnes and asked them to bring everything they had on Janet Gray.

"What do you think?" he asked twenty minutes later after they had made a timetable of Janet Gray's activities during the time in question.

"Murder her own daughter?" said Agnes.

Keegan shrugged. "Straddle indicted him for it. If father, then mother."

"He's not the father."

"Come on."

Agnes laid it out for him, the date of the birth of Sonya, the public record of the liaison between Janet and Chris, the fact that Bourke had been in Rome prowling around the edges of the last session of the Council, making outrageous statements for sympathetic newsmen about the tragicomic life of celibate priests. Given the birth date, Bourke was in Italy when the baby was conceived.

"Maybe she was born early."

"An eight-pound preemie?"

"Not likely?"

"Maybe for rhinos. How naive a guy was he?"

Keegan had the disturbing thought that many men could be deceived in the way Agnes was suggesting. Who is going to think the baby his new wife is carrying is not his?

"This is all circumstantial, of course. But tests could be made with the samples the coroner has."

"Any idea who the father might be?"

"I have a guess."

Among the things Agnes had come up with when she asked for a clipping search on both Christopher Bourke and Janet Gray was a number of stories on the then-young nun's compassionate concern for the convicts in the prison at Joliet. Sister Mary Chrysostom had taken this as her special apostolate, with the approval of her superiors, and spent a good deal of time at the prison. She became particularly concerned with the plight of one man, Jason Nagy. There were fading photographs of the two, a youthful and attractive Janet looking soulfully into the camera; beside her the frowning, thick-browed prisoner. Janet had developed the theory that Nagy had been tried and convicted without really knowing what was going on. He was a Hungarian refugee, his English imperfect, he was, she suggested, a casualty of a system too eager to rush to judgment. Apparently she was right. The conviction was reviewed and thrown out, no new trial was scheduled, and Nagy was almost smiling in the photograph showing him leaving the courthouse with Janet hanging on his arm.

"She never went back to the convent. That is the period when she would have become pregnant. Look at this."

Agnes put another clipping before him. Nagy's wife arriving from Budapest for a reunion with her husband.

"I think she turned to Bourke on the rebound."

"And Sonya is Nagy's daughter."

"I think so."

"What does it mean?"

"You're the captain," Agnes said, scooping up her materials, obviously pleased with herself.

"Leave those here, will you?"

She gave him a salute. There was one damned good detective, Keegan told himself, wondering what in the world to make of what she had dug up.

"I wonder how old the guy would be now if he is still alive."

"Something like seventy. He's been back in jail in the meantime, twice for beating his wife. She went back to Hungary. He operated a freight elevator for the Zecker Company."

"Where are they?"

"He worked in their warehouse."

The warehouse was two blocks from the EH warehouse, a block from where Tuttle had parked his car. Keegan looked at Cy. "Let's talk to him."

"Shall I go along?" Agnes asked.

"It's still your case, isn't it?"

ROGER DOWLING, when Keegan rang him up, was not in, and Marie Murkin was a little touchy about admitting it.

"Where did he go?"

"Philip Keegan, if I telephoned your office and you weren't there and I asked where you were, what would you think of that?"

"If I weren't there, I wouldn't think a thing."

"You know what I mean."

"Where is he?"

"I don't know."

"Well, if you don't want to tell me, don't."

"I mean it. He was here and then he wasn't."

"Probably over in church."

"I looked."

"The school?"

"I called over there."

"When did you last see him?"

"Oh, for heaven's sake, he is not a missing person."

"You're the one who brought it up. Maybe I'll drop by."

Kidding with Marie brought back some of the joys of married life. He hadn't had a really good argument since his wife died. Not that he intended to get married again. God forbid. Still, it was nice to have Marie Murkin to tease when he dropped in to see his old friend Father Dowling.

THIRTY

EARLIER THAT AFTERNOON, in his study, Roger Dowling had been, despite himself, reviewing the events of the past weeks and, as he brought a match to his pipe, what seemed very much like an epiphany came. The thought that occurred to him was so obvious he was almost wary of it. Surely, it would have occurred to Phil and Cy and their cohorts. But it was from talking to Maud that the thought had come. He realized that Phil and Cy did not have access to information that had come his way.

Sonya kidnapped and her body stuffed in the back seat of Tuttle's car while the lawyer was lured to the EH warehouse.

Craig Wilhelms found dead behind the wheel of his car parked in his garage, an apparent suicide, but the odd business with the door suggesting otherwise.

The two were linked with EH, with Chris and Janet. They were also linked to the fact that they both had gotten religion, were drawn to Catholicism, and apparently, if Katie Powell was right, to one another too.

Janet had an affair with Craig, one that broke up his marriage. Chris had cavorted with Loraine Howells. But neither dalliance lay outside the common creed of this strange couple; random coupling was to be ex-

pected, fidelity to one's spouse rejected as a con-
straint on freedom. Despite that, the two had
obviously come to hate one another. Janet wanted a
divorce; and worse, far worse—she spoke of returning to the convent she had deserted when she married
Chris. At the time she had apparently already been
with child by Nagy, a fact that could not leave Chris
indifferent, no matter what theory he professed.

Now Chris had confessed to the murders of his
daughter—at least of Janet's daughter—and of Craig
as well. Yet it seemed clear that he could have committed neither crime. It was not simply that Loraine
said he had been with her at the time Sonya was killed;
Cy Horvath could attest to it.

Janet had told Amos Cadbury that Chris's confession was meant to throw suspicion on her when it became clear that Chris could not have done what he
claimed to do.

Roger Dowling had pondered these developments
and the revelations by this cast of characters. He had
tried to dismiss his epiphany, but before the lawyer's
arrival, he sat for a moment; then he nodded, picked
up the phone, and dialed. Nothing Amos had said
made Father Dowling regret that he had made that
call.

"DO YOU MIND if we just drive around in the van?"
Barney asked Roger Dowling when the pastor went to
the front door. Roger had been awaiting his guest.

He had identified himself as Maud's son but Roger
would have known him from half a mile away. Not

many could fit the description Maud had given him of her thirty-nine-year-old boy. The van Barney referred to stood up the street, near the school, and it seemed to list to one side. Roger remembered Maud remarking how proud he was of owning that vehicle.

"Sure."

He closed the door behind him. No need to go back and tell Marie he was going out. He didn't have to inform her of his every move. Too bad she hadn't answered the door when Barney came. The man had to be seen to be believed. Barney was already on his way to the van, and long before Roger caught up, he was holding open its flimsy front door.

The van was a battered old VW that had the look of a vehicle that had seen the worst of several continents. A far cry from the stretch limousine Christopher Bourke came calling in. That seemed a harmless topic to get started on when he was buckled in and Barney had pulled away.

"Do you know what a stretch limo is?"

"Why?"

Barney seemed a serious fellow and he concentrated on his driving. His beard did not lie flat on his face but stood out electrically. The baseball cap gave him a youthful appearance, but Roger Dowling realized that Maud's boy was no longer a boy.

"No reason. Someone came calling for me in one a while ago. It was quite a different ride than this one."

"I know."

"Did you see the Cubs last night?"

"I don't follow baseball."

"Well, at least you know they're a baseball team."

He was not an easy man to have a conversation with, but then driving the van was a full-time occupation. Barney hunched bearlike over the wheel, as if tacking into the wind. Perhaps the wheels were out of alignment.

"Why did you want to see me?"

"It was your mother who suggested we talk."

"It was Bourke who came in the limo," Barney said.

"That's right."

"What do you think of him as a priest?"

"What do I as a priest think of him? Or what sort of priest do I think he is? He's a layman now."

"What do you think of him as a layman?"

"The lost shepherd is always a sad sight."

"He's worse than a lost shepherd."

"I guess you're right. Do you know why your mother wanted us to talk?"

He straightened the bill of his baseball cap. "She's always worried about the wrong things."

"You?"

"She should have worried more about Loraine."

"Your cousin?"

"That's right, my cousin. Christopher Bourke's girlfriend."

He spoke with sudden vehemence. "The harm that man has done!"

"Your mother worries because she didn't bring you up as a Catholic."

"I've got nothing against Catholics."

"You should be one."

"Does she want you to convert me?"

"Maybe."

"So go ahead."

Roger Dowling laughed. Such conversations are difficult in any circumstances, but in the swaying noisy van it would have been impossible. There was something to be said for stretch limousines.

"Why don't we stop somewhere?"

"We're nearly there."

"Where are we going?"

"Where I work."

"And where's that?"

"A warehouse."

Barney turned off Austin and thumped across some railroad tracks and then through a blighted area where rusting steel frames of buildings, their sides gone, created a ghost-town effect in the middle of Chicago. It was difficult to reconcile this landscape with the pride in Barney's voice when he said their destination was where he worked. But now they were on a well-paved street flanked by warehouses, with ribbons of tended lawn in front of them. Barney turned in at one, pressed a gadget, and a door began to lift. Half a minute later they were inside and the door was closing behind them.

"Wait," Barney said. "I'll get the light."

Roger Dowling waited in the dark. Once the door had gone down, there was no source of light at all. The overhead lamp went on and Roger opened the door and eased himself out of the van.

"I'm here."

Barney stood at a propped-open door and the priest could see the office within. He joined Barney and soon they were in the small, brightly lit room where Barney earned his bread. The chair behind the desk looked like a settee, but nothing less would have accommodated Barney's girth. He lowered himself into the chair, took off his cap and put it on the desk.

"Welcome to the inner sanctum, Father."

"Very nice."

"Not all the comforts of a limo, but nice enough for a good talk."

"Perfect."

"Why did Bourke come see you?"

"We knew one another long ago," Roger Dowling said after a moment. He did not like the question. "You're very interested in him, aren't you, Barney?"

"I'm interested in you too." He paused. "Do I have to call you Father?"

"Whatever you like."

"You know a lot of police, don't you? And lawyers?"

"Have you been spying on me?"

The room seemed almost airtight suddenly. Barney's great impassive face told Roger Dowling little, but the epiphany he had had seemed even more obvious than it had at first. If indeed Barney was linked to Sonya, to Craig Wilhelms, to... But he had detected dread in Maud's voice.

"How much do you know?"

"About what?"

Barney rolled sideways in his chair to draw a hand-
kerchief from his pocket. He blew his nose with gusto,
staring at Roger Dowling as he did. It seemed a species of Bronx cheer.

"You seem remarkably philosophical about Christopher Bourke, Father Dowling."

"Whatever I think of him, there's very little I can do
about it."

"That is not my view of the matter."

"What is your view?"

Barney picked up his cap, looked at it, and smiled.
"Is this why you asked about the Cubs?" He put
down the cap. "The more I thought about it, the more
it seemed to me that a man like that should not go unpunished. If someone scattered garbage around the
neighborhood, he would be at least arrested and fined.
If the garbage caused illnesses, even deaths, the punishment would be more severe. Bourke and his wife fill
the air with something worse than garbage."

"That's true."

"Imagine celebrating hedonism in a society that is
dying of it already."

Roger Dowling sat back. He patted his pockets but
without hope. He had not thought to bring pipe and
tobacco with him. "Is that a coffeepot?"

"Later. Let's get it onto the table. How did you
suspect?"

It seemed best to keep silent. Roger had a sudden
realization that he was enclosed in a remote strange
environment with a very odd young man and that no
one knew where he was.

"Going undetected was not high on my agenda, though I would of course prefer not to be arrested for performing a public service."

"I'm not following you, Barney."

"There was no torture involved. That's important. The girl was no more guilty than Isaac when Abraham was prepared to sacrifice him. I misled her biblically as to what was happening. She didn't really understand until the last moment, and then it was over. She was sitting in the chair you're in."

"Sonya."

"I went to the coffeepot behind there and then . . ." He pulled open the desk drawer and drew forth a needlelike length of steel. One end was taped, the other sharpened to a point. "My thrust was accurate. There was very little blood. Death was instantaneous."

"Why did you kill her?"

"God keeps a set of books, Father Dowling. Debits and credits. The sins of the father are visited on the children. I did not invent the system. I am simply its minister."

It would have been convenient to think him mad, but there was a simplicity in the enormous young man that must have rendered Sonya unsuspecting until it was too late. He had sought to put the body into Craig's car, but Craig had appeared with his secretary. Barney followed them to the warehouse and after the secretary drove off, put the body in Tuttle's car. "God's ways are not our ways," he said, smiling oddly.

Barney was eager to tell his story now. Clearly he thought Roger Dowling's invitation to the rectory had been prompted by his surveillance, as if the pastor were aware of Barney's monitoring the comings and goings at the rectory. Barney would suspect the suspicious. Phil Keegan and Cy Horvath, both frequent visitors, must have seemed more than meaningful to him. No wonder the priest wanted to lure him to the rectory. He talked with eerie ease about it. He had seen the frantic parents on television, announcing the disappearance of their daughter.

"I knew I had made a good beginning. Job was tested first by the loss of possessions, then by the loss of his children, then the Lord permitted Satan to afflict Job himself. There seemed little point in worrying about his possessions. When I had completed my task they would be of no use to him."

"Craig Wilhelms?"

"That was aimed at both of them, but particularly her. No surprise that she should sleep with someone other than her husband, of course. It's what they've been telling other people to do for years. Give them credit for consistency."

"You feel that strongly about them?"

"Why should that surprise a priest?"

"You killed Sonya." He was uncomfortably conscious of the seat in which he sat. "And Craig Wilhelms. How do you think a priest would react to that. And Our Lord?"

Barney nodded in approval. "If I were acting in my own name, I would of course be a murderer. Was Abraham a murderer?"

There seemed little point in saying that God had stayed Abraham's hand, since that might seem to concede Barney's claim to be God's agent. It was almost a diversion to hear how he had killed Craig Wilhelms.

"I meant to bring him here, but he refused and I subdued him. After I put him in the car and started the motor I took the remote control and closed the garage door from where I was parked across the street."

"And opened it again when the paperboy came?"

His shoulders rose and fell. Laughter? It had taken two tries. The first time the kid didn't notice the door going up.

Roger Dowling raised his brows receptively. A red second hand moved with slow inexorability around a large round clock behind Barney. The only sounds audible in that room were the sounds in the room. They could have been in a space capsule, or a tomb. Seated behind his desk, Barney, who had seemed half-comical and inept when he came to the rectory door, now looked very serious and solemn, in command of the world as he saw it. Had working in this room, out of connection with day or night or other people, fed his imagination? On the desktop lay a large Jerusalem Bible, obviously very much read. He was speaking of Loraine.

"Your cousin."

"The victim of Christopher Bourke. You know of course the etymology of Christopher."

"Yes."

"Irony of irony. He is a Christ taker-away, not bearer. Whilst my mother worried about me, her darling Loraine was being seduced and corrupted by this man. She was devoting her talents to the success of that degrading enterprise. Enlightened Hedonism! You might as well say laundered filth."

"So it was your cousin who provided your motivation."

He pressed back against his chair. "The occasion, not the motivation. The motivation came from God. My position is of course a difficult one. Imagine Abraham explaining to the neighbors that God commanded him to sacrifice Isaac. He knows it's true. We accept it as true. But the neighbors?" He leaned forward. "I have no illusions about my eventual lot, Roger Dowling."

"It is wise to make all this known now."

"But my mission is not complete."

"You have done enough."

"Get thee behind me, Satan! There are still the principals. Janet and Christopher themselves. I have been moving gradually toward them. Their attention has been gained, fears will have begun, they must be wondering what comes next."

"Chris Bourke has confessed to the two murders."

"God is not mocked."

"Janet is seeking a divorce, she wants to return—"

"No! It is too late. They have led others to hell, why should they now escape the just judgment for what they have done?"

"I think we should leave that to God."

"Exactly! And I am his instrument."

"Why have you told me all this?"

"Is it really news, Father?"

"You see me as a threat?"

"Not if you accept my commission to do what I am doing."

Delude him? Lie to him? Humor him? "I have a commission of my own, Barney. You must not continue in this way..."

"You would have Sonya and Craig die and those two escape?"

"That is not quite the decision I face. Barney, why don't you and I go back to the rectory? Captain Keegan, as you must have guessed, is an old friend of mine. I'll ask him to come and we'll talk this thing out."

Barney's smile pressed into his cheeks. "Nice try, Padre. But I guess that answers my question. I can't let you walk out of here."

Sitting facing a man who had admitted to killing two people and planned to kill two more, Roger Dowling felt for a moment the fatalistic sensation that came over him whenever a plane he was on first took off into the air. Tons and tons of complicated machinery and hundreds of human souls hung momentarily in the balance, defying gravity, suspended as from a spider's thread from the will of God. Was he destined to have his life end in this hermetically sealed warehouse office? He put his hands on the arms of his chair and rose to his feet.

"Aristotle left Athens because he did not want the Athenians to sin against philosophy a second time."

"Sit down, Father. That door is locked, it is the only way out."

"I feel already buried in here."

"I think of it as my cell. It is a monastic existence. My tasks are few. It gives me time for the Lord." He laid a large hand on the Bible.

"I have work to do as well."

"And you will get to it, Father, if you do not fight against Providence. I have no wish to harm you. There was a time when Chris Bourke seemed somehow to be involving you in his schemes, when I thought you too might be included in the object of the Lord's wrath. But I have no instructions in your regard. Nonetheless, I cannot allow anything to deter me. If you left here now, you would doubtless call your friend Captain Keegan. You would feel obliged to. I cannot risk that. You are going to have to stay here until I have completed what I have begun."

THIRTY-ONE

JANET GRAY AGREED to be interviewed but only with her lawyer present, and Amos Cadbury asked Captain Keegan if it couldn't be done in his chambers.

"My client has been through a good deal lately, and her ordeal may have just begun."

Maybe only a manner of speaking, with Cadbury you never knew, but Phil was glad to have Cadbury there when he asked Janet Gray if she remembered a man named Nagy. It was immediately clear that she did, but she said nothing, looking straight at him. Her expression did not change when she said, "No."

"This would have been a long time ago."

"I don't remember the name."

"This was when you were still a nun, of course, and were working with men in prison."

"Captain, what are you getting at?"

"It got into the papers at the time, your helping Nagy. Thanks to you he was granted a new trial, but the prosecutor chose not to pursue it."

"What about him?"

"You remember him now?"

She looked at Amos Cadbury, as if he should be preventing such questions, but he nodded gravely, giving his approval that she should answer. That wasn't what she wanted at all.

"Does it really make any difference whether I remember him? Apparently you have been checking old newspaper reports."

"Has he been in contact with you lately?"

"No! Why should he be?"

"Mrs. Bourke, you have to understand that these questions are difficult for me to ask."

"Oh, you have my sympathy," she said sharply. "What a dreadful job you have."

"What was the birth date of your daughter Sonya?"

"My daughter! Mr. Cadbury, do I have to tolerate this? I see no rhyme nor reason in what he is saying."

"The suggestion has been made that Christopher Bourke could not have been the father of your daughter." Keegan held up his hand like a traffic cop. "The suggestion has been made that Nagy had time and opportunity."

Janet Gray rose and brought her bag around in a great looping arc, a bolero move, but Keegan easily fended it off. Amos Cadbury rose to take his client's arm. He looked sternly at Phil Keegan.

"Captain, I have no idea what basis you might have for your extraordinary remarks, moreover I fail to see that they have anything to do with the purpose of this interview. Either connect them or desist from further questions."

"I have two questions. Did Nagy know he was the father? Did Bourke know Nagy was the father?"

"Captain, the presuppositions of those questions—"

"Answer them," Amos Cadbury said.

"No," said Janet Gray, in a cold, controlled voice. "No to both questions. Is that all you wanted to know?"

"You answer with great confidence. I take that to mean you have no reason to think either of them knew. I ask you to think for a moment. Has anything happened of late that could cause you to doubt your certainty?"

"Like what?"

"I have no idea."

She did give it thought, although she clearly was anxious to have this interview behind her. Her answer to his further question was another no.

Phil would have called it quits then but Amos Cadbury asked Janet to expand on her answers, and on the presupposition to the questions. "This is not of course idle curiosity, Mrs. Bourke. A counselor is more effective in proportion to the knowledge he has of his case and client, however remote and irrelevant that knowledge may seem."

Phil remained as what Agnes Lamb would call a resource person, but he would be able to take away Janet Gray's admission that Nagy had fathered her child and she had never told Christopher about it. Amos explored this last point with great delicacy, establishing without explicitly saying it that Janet had married Christopher Bourke to avoid the shame of an unwed pregnancy. That she had still technically been a nun at the time was never mentioned but seemed to have been shouted into the room as they talked. When it was over, Phil was passing through the reception area when the brittle, juiceless receptionist, Miss Cleary, snapped her fingers. He turned and she pointed at the phone she was holding.

"One moment, sir," she said to the phone and then held the instrument out to Phil Keegan.

"Captain Keegan? Amos Cadbury. I am glad Miss Cleary caught you before you left the office. I have Marie Murkin on the line and I think it would be well if you spoke with her."

"Put her on."

The narrowed eyes of Miss Cleary looked through him. "And thank you, Amos," Phil said and Miss Cleary spun away in outraged indignation at this presumptuous good fellowship. Phil guessed that she called him Mr. Cadbury even in the privacy of her mind. And then Marie came on the phone.

"Phil Keegan, I am going out of my mind. Father Dowling has walked off and I've no idea where he is. I should have told you this when you called earlier. I am sure that something is wrong."

"Why?"

"He never does this. He always tells me when he's going out."

"How long's he been gone?"

"I don't know!"

"When did you last see him?"

He dragged the conversation on, if only to annoy Miss Cleary, who sat in frozen disapproval as he used her telephone for this idiotic exchange. He told Marie Murkin to get hold of herself, he would check with her over the next hour or so, everything was going to be all right. "He's a big boy, Marie."

When he replaced the receiver, Miss Cleary snatched the phone from him. Amos Cadbury's door opened and he conducted Janet Gray through the reception area. Miss Cleary made a great display of not noticing.

"Captain," Cadbury said, after his client was gone, "would you come back to my office a moment?"

"Of course, Amos."

The already ramrod back of the lawyer stiffened at this familiarity but he continued to walk. Keegan winked at Miss Cleary, whose mouth had dropped open at this sacrilege.

"Marie Murkin told me of Father Dowling's absence before I turned her over to you. I wonder if I didn't see something when I left the rectory earlier that may be of significance."

"Like what?"

"When did she last see Father Dowling?"

"She's not sure. Not during the past three hours."

"Aha. I visited the rectory earlier, and when I left I noticed a very large young man get out of a van and go up to the rectory door."

"Someone you knew?"

"Oh no. But I was struck by the incongruity. He did not have the look of a parishioner."

"A repairman."

"I suppose that's the explanation, although his clothing... Forgive me, Captain. I'm afraid something of Marie's alarm has rubbed off on me."

"What repairman?" Marie demanded twenty minutes later. "There was no repairman here. There is nothing to be repaired. Why do you ask?"

"Did you know Mr. Cadbury was here today?" He blew on his coffee and then sipped it.

"Captain Keegan, I know who visits the rectory."

"Who was the fat young man?"

"What fat young man?"

"Who visited the rectory."

Marie slumped at the kitchen table, her wide eyes watering as she looked at him. "Something's happened, hasn't it? Something happened and you don't want to tell me."

THIRTY-TWO

"CHRIS? There's a call on one I think you should take."

"Something you can't handle?"

Recent events had altered Loraine, and Christopher Bourke was not sure he liked the change. If he had been told that he liked his employees obsequious, deferential, subservient, he would have dismissed the suggestion with a laugh. He prided himself on his common touch, the ability to reach out to where people lived and move them. He'd had that knack when he was a priest as well.

"This is something only you can handle."

"Sure." He punched one. "Christopher Bourke."

After several seconds a whispery voice spoke. "I'm calling on behalf of Roger Dowling. Father Dowling."

"Who is this?"

"He has asked me to telephone you and ask if you would come here."

"To the rectory?" Bourke had seen only Marie Murkin when he visited Roger Dowling. Was this one of the old duffers who hung around the parish school, putting in time until he got the big send-off with a requiem Mass?

"I'll come for you. Your car is too showy."

"Is that right? Who's speaking?"

But the line went dead. "Up yours, buddy," Bourke said half-aloud. The door opened and Loraine looked in.

"Weird?"

"Did you listen in?"

She nodded. "And taped it."

Her suspicion had the odd effect of allaying his own. He resented her suggestion that she could antic-ipate his thoughts, know in advance what he might or might not think. Besides, he owed Roger one. What if the man was ill? What if he was turning to his old friend in his capacity as a priest? He sat back, tuning out Loraine, staring at the stippled ceiling. He had the sudden claustrophobic feeling he'd had sitting in the confessional, semi-dark, the grille lined with a pulpy layer meant to soften the sounds of sinners and con-fessor. How he had hated those priestly tasks before he had the sense to go. Mumbling the words of the Mass, ripping through the Breviary, the Latin words an end-less unintelligible flow, the intention was the thing. And weddings. At weddings he was assailed by raun-chy thoughts of what the two bright-faced people be-fore him would be doing a few hours after he had declared them man and wife. This plea from Roger threatened to suck him back into all that, but of course he no longer believed a word of it—that what he whispered to a penitent washed away sins, that words of his turned bread and wine into the body and blood of Jesus. His unbelief wouldn't matter, of course. For

Roger's purposes he would be a priest like any other, ordained, bearing an indelible mark into eternity.

He sent Loraine to the studio, something she interpreted to mean that he was dismissing the phone call, then went into the foyer, whose glass walls looked onto the street. The man on the phone had not said when he would come, but the urgency in his voice suggested it would be immediately. The drive from St. Hilary's was at least twenty minutes. He should have stayed in his office.

The battered van that came groping up the drive might have been that of a confused delivery man, but the big man behind the wheel was looking intently around, as if he expected someone to be there. Was this his ride? Chris was reaching for the door when his name was called. Loraine hurried across the foyer to him.

"I've been waiting in the studio."

"My ride is here."

A confused expression came over her face and then she looked past him to the van outside. Bourke pulled open the door and skipped down the steps to the now-opened passenger door.

"Christopher Bourke," he said, putting out his hand. But the driver was too busy pulling into traffic. Bourke turned to see Loraine standing in the foyer, hands on hips, her head tipped to one side.

"What's wrong with Father Dowling?"

"I'm not a doctor."

"My God. Is he ill?"

"He asked for you."

"Do you know who I am?"

"He said you were a priest."

Bourke relaxed. His hunches were seldom wrong. But it was unseemly to feel relief because a stricken Roger Dowling had sent for him in his hour of need. How eerie it had been as a young priest, anointing the dying, watching them drift into the great unknown, reassured by the presence of a priest who knew no more than they did of what lay ahead for them. If anything. He had seen more dead people in the first half year as a priest than he had in his lifetime before. How dead the dead are. The embalmer's arts were needed to stay the dissolution of the flesh, but soon in any case there would be rot, then dust, then crumbling bones, then nothing. The resurrection of the body presupposed a body but bodies do not survive.

Bouncing around on the seat, which seemed to hang over the road they went along, Chris grabbed the seat belt and brought it across his body.

"The latch don't work."

By the time the driver said this, Chris had discovered this for himself. He got a good grip on the handle above the door.

"What's your name?"

"Barney."

"Just Barney?"

"Bernard, actually."

"You got a last name?"

"Kaiser."

It sounded familiar, but he dealt with so many half-remembered names. He did not have to use his memory for such things; assistants whispered in his ear, slipped him notes, made smooth his way.

"What's your relation to Father Dowling?"

"Just another sinner." The man grinned under the bill of his baseball cap.

"How was he when you left him?"

"Anxious to see you."

"Is this as fast as this thing goes?"

Barney stomped down on the gas pedal, but this had little effect on their progress. They seemed to be taking an odd route, but that was another thing Bourke was used to having others do, carry him from place to place. He seldom noticed how he got to where he was going. But this guy was no Eddie, that was for sure.

Eddie. Anger stirred in him when he thought of what Eddie had been doing, taping what went on in the passenger compartment. Why? He hadn't tried blackmail, but no doubt that would have come eventually. What a rat. But what was Eddie compared to Janet? He should have had a contingency plan, a way of easing her out of the spotlight, but she appealed to certain types, and it would have seemed crazy to decrease the attractiveness of EH. For years he had been thinking of ways to expand, grow bigger and better. Bouncing around in the old VW van, he felt suddenly tired. The thing seemed to be unraveling of itself. Sonya. Craig. Maybe this was the time to close it down, get out, take it easy. How much money did he need, for God's sake? Even if he had to split it down the middle with Janet, there was a king's ransom left.

Thirty pieces of silver.

He tried to push the thought away but it kept coming back, bouncing with the movement of the van. The desire to repent, go back, be told she was a good girl and would spend eternity in heaven had finally gotten to Janet. She couldn't possibly believe that, but faith isn't always necessary. Wanting to believe suffices. And Janet wanted desperately to believe.

I would have to pretend, he told himself. Make believe. It wouldn't be so hard. What else had he been doing these past years? Pretending that a roll in the hay was ecstasy. It seldom was, and even so, how much time was involved? Minutes? Seconds? And you couldn't keep it up, you had to recover. It was a silly thing to put at the center of life, yet once he had really believed that was the solution.

And once he had believed he had the power to give a sinner absolution. He might be about to do that for Roger Dowling.

"I don't know this route."

"Neither did Father Dowling."

"I don't understand."

"He fell ill in my office. That's where we're going."

"Your office! I thought we were going to St. Hilary's."

"A natural mistake. I said Father Dowling."

"Where the hell is your office?"

"Right here."

And he swung the van to the left, tipping Bourke off balance. Geez, the door could have popped open and he'd be rolling in the street. He would be glad to hand himself down to solid earth.

"This way."

Up a flight of stairs and through a door and into darkness.

"What is this place?"

"A warehouse." The light went on. "This way."

Bourke went through the door and there was Roger Dowling tied up in a chair, an apologetic expression on his face. The door closed and Bourke turned to see the fat man locking it. Too late he realized he had been sucked into a trap.

THIRTY-THREE

CHRIS'S REALIZATION that he had been tricked was written all over his face when he appeared in the doorway and looked at Roger Dowling. But he was passive only for a moment. With a sudden move of his arm, he jammed his elbow into Barney's massive stomach, wheeled and swung his right arm in a wide arc, but before his fist made contact with the fat man, Barney grabbed his arm, wrenched it as he pushed his way into the office and then brought the arm behind Chris's back and levered it upward, bringing a scream of pain from Bourke's contorted face. Barney flung Chris into a corner, tried the door to make sure it was locked, and sank with a sigh into the chair behind the desk.

"You son of a bitch," Chris growled. He half-lay, half-sat, his shoulder jammed against the wall.

Barney ignored him, looked concernedly at Roger Dowling.

"I got back as quickly as I could. When I catch my breath, I'll untie you."

"Roger," Chris said, trying to get control of his voice, "what in the name of God is going on?"

"I'm not in charge, I'm afraid."

"You were essential, Father Dowling, as you can

see. You were the bait that enabled me to land the big fish. But what does one do with used bait?''

"I suppose you'll have to kill us both," Roger Dowling said evenly.

The thought seemed to sadden Barney. "Fortunately, that's not true. I do not expect the world to understand the nature of my actions. That is between God and myself. After I have fulfilled my mission, I will be subject to the Prince of This World." Barney tipped his head, as if listening for some mystical demur. Hearing none, he nodded. "No. Father Dowling, you will go free after I have done what I must do.''

"What the hell is he talking about?"

Barney's large head turned slowly toward Chris. "Watch your tongue, you sinner. You shall not escape the wrath of God. The time in which you might have repented is past.''

"That's not for you to say, Barney."

"True, Father Dowling. It is not for me to say. And it is not I who speak.''

How long had it been since Barney collapsed into his chair? Not long enough, Roger Dowling calculated. He must temporize.

"What about Janet Gray, Barney?"

The fat man dipped his head when he looked at Dowling. "She too has incurred the wrath of the Lord.''

"But she will go unpunished."

Barney shook his head, his eyes remaining fixed on Roger Dowling. Roger spelled it out for him.

"You sacrifice Chris, but then you set me free and, you say, deliver yourself up to the police. They are not likely to accept your version of events. You will go to prison. And Janet Gray will go unpunished."

Chris, in a crouch now, followed this exchange with a look of disbelief on his face. The last five or ten minutes could have had no precedent in his previous life. Gulled into coming to this warehouse, perhaps out of the first altruistic feeling in years, he had been manhandled, told he was about to die, and now heard Roger Dowling chiding Barney for failing to ensure that Janet Gray too should die.

"What do you suggest, Father Dowling?" Barney asked suspiciously.

Roger rose to his feet, taking the rope he had arranged around his body again before Barney returned. Barney watched this in surprise.

"You untied yourself."

"That's right. I held my breath and expanded my chest when you tied me. You would never make a sailor, Barney, with knots like those. And now it's your turn."

He held up the rope. He had turned it into a lasso. Surprise gave way to anger. Barney got up, or at least tried to. The chair stuck firmly to his bottom as he tried to rise. Standing stooped, he grabbed the arms of the chair, and that was when Roger Dowling dropped the loop over him and pulled it tight, binding Barney's arms to his side. Chris jumped up and rushed across the room and helped Roger wind the rope around the squirming, bellowing Barney, who could not free himself from his chair. But it was no easy matter to immobilize the huge man. When they had, Roger said, "Do you want to go for help or should I?"

"I'd say you've done pretty well on your own. How did you do it?"

"His chair? Epoxy glue. Go call the police, Chris."

THIRTY-FOUR

FORSYTHIA HAD GIVEN WAY to lilacs and peonies, and now roses bloomed along the walk between the rectory and the church. Marie Murkin had come outside to cut some roses for the May altar in her room when she saw the tragic figure of Maud Kaiser slip into the church. The poor woman. Her son had killed two people and would have killed more if he hadn't been stopped by Father Dowling. The woman's gratitude to the pastor of St. Hilary's brought her often to the parish.

"It's really the bingo that draws her," Father Dowling said.

He could never be serious, not when there was any danger that he would get credit for what he had done. Honestly, the newspapers made it sound as if Christopher Bourke had rescued him! The renegade priest had not discouraged this interpretation and Father Dowling would not listen when Marie urged him to make the record clear.

"Marie, all I did was glue a man to his chair. I stole it from the Three Stooges."

"And tied up a killer single-handed!"

If Phil Keegan hadn't told her, Marie herself might have thought it was Chris Bourke who had been the hero. Barney Kaiser had raged at this interference in the Lord's plan of vengeance.''

"He sounds like someone in the bible," Marie said, shivering. Roger had the unnerving thought that she might think real prophets were as crazy as Barney.

He was judged incompetent to stand trial, getting better treatment than biblical prophets. Weekly letters to the pastor of St. Hilary's arrived from the state hospital where Barney was interned, lamentations, anathemas, messages Barney was passing on from the Lord.

"I saw the man go into the rectory when I was leaving," Amos Cadbury told Roger Dowling afterward. "I had a feeling there was something strange about him. That is why I mentioned it to Captain Keegan."

Marie sought no credit for sounding the alarm herself. She was willing to get her reward in the next world. But who would have thought Amos Cadbury would try to steal the limelight?

He had obtained a divorce for Janet Gray and she had said good-bye to the world in which for twenty years she had been a cause of scandal and consternation to many. Her daughter was dead, she wanted to spend the rest of her life in reparation for the harm she had done. Chris Bourke, seizing the role of hero Tetzel thrust upon him, let Janet go without a fight, but then she made no claim on their common fortune. A happy ending for the loathsome ex-priest? Not if the IRS had their way. The publicity had drawn the skeptical eye of investigators to EH, and Tetzel, who would not name his sources, said the government was proceeding on information from inside the organization.

"Loraine," Maud told Roger Dowling. "The girl's as fierce as Barney about it."

A woman scorned. But Marie found herself thinking of Nagy, apparently the father of Sonya. When Cy Horvath and Agnes showed up at his place of work to question him, the man suffered a heart attack. He was now recovering from triple bypass surgery. Marie frowned. Such language. It reminded her of the awful interstates that now looped about Fox River. It was dread of returning to prison rather than news of the daughter he had never known, had never known he had, that explained the attack. Agnes and Cy had probably saved the man's life, caring for him until the paramedics arrived.

Inside, Marie climbed the stairs to her room and arranged the roses before the statue of Our Lady. She whispered the Memorare and then descended to the kitchen to prepare the luncheon Father Dowling would have when he returned from saying the noon Mass. Phil Keegan came with him.

"Barney's mother was there," Phil spoke to the pastor.

"Yes, I noticed."

"How's he doing?"

"Would you like to read his latest letter?"

"What's he have to say?"

Roger Dowling looked up from his fettucini. "He made more sense before he became unglued."

CRIMINALS ALWAYS HAVE SOMETHING TO HIDE—BUT THE ENJOYMENT YOU'LL GET OUT OF A WORLDWIDE MYSTERY NOVEL IS NO SECRET....

With Worldwide Mystery on the case, we've taken the mystery out of finding something good to read every month.

Worldwide Mystery is guaranteed to have suspense buffs and chill seekers of all persuasions in eager pursuit of each new exciting title!

Worldwide Mystery novels—crimes worth
investigating...

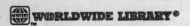 **WORLDWIDE LIBRARY®**